Asleep in the Nightmare Room

T.J. Tranchell

Blysster Press

Email the author at: tj@warning-signs.net

Website: www.warning-signs.net
Facebook: www.facebook.com/TJTranchell

"Asleep in the Nightmare Room" Printing History
Blysster Press print history: June 2017

Blysster Press

A new kind of publisher for a new kind of world.

ISBN 978-1-940247-34-2

Printed in the United States of America
www.blysster.com

To
The writers, artists, and filmmakers
Who helped make me the writer I am today
And for Pic.

THANK YOU

For this collection, I need to acknowledge my teachers: John Ziebell, Brandon Schrand, Jeff Jones, Shawn O'Neal, Katherine Whitcomb, Lisa Norris, Liahna Armstrong, Laila Abdalla, Joe Johnson, Xavier Cavazos, and George Drake.

Thanks also go to all of my students over the last two years at the University of Idaho Student Media. There are too many of you to thank individually, but your support is invaluable.

To my early readers: Ryan Bailey and Alisa Hoag. So many commas.

To all of my fellow 2017 Borderlands Press Boot Camp grunts: We're all in this together.

Again, to my family, especially all of you who bought *Cry Down Dark*, even if you never read it.

My appreciation for the faith and support given me by my publisher Blysster Press and Charity Becker is beyond words.

Special thanks to Sue Stevens and Steve Cummings whose guest room inspired this title.

Finally, as always, I can't thank my wife Savannah and son Clark enough for what they mean to me.

Grateful acknowledgment to the places that previously published many of the contents you now hold:

"Bury All Your Secrets in My Skin," *Disturbed Digest #13*, Alban Lake Publishing, June 2016.

"Dead Again Tomorrow," *Nitebalde*, March 2009.

"Hemingway at Work," *Mad Scientist Journal*, February 2014.

"Nail Shitter," *Despumation Vol. 1*, Despumation Press, May 2014.

"Nutjob," *GIVE: An Anthology of Anatomical Entries*, When the Dead Books, May 2015.

"Pool," *Manastash Vol. 25*, Central Washington University, May 2015.

"Scream Queen" partially appeared in *Cry Down Dark*, Blysster Press, March 2016.

"Seeds and All," *Westering Vol. 3*, College of Southern Nevada, April 2005.

"The Show Begins at 10:31," originally appeared on Matchflick.com, February-August 2009.

"Voices Carry," *Holiday Horror 2014*, TJ Weeks Books, January 2014 and as "Just One Night," *Westering Vol. 2*, College of Southern Nevada, September 2004.

Table of Contents

Asleep in the Nightmare Room

The earliest nightmare I can remember was about a spider. Maybe yours was, too. Or perhaps your earliest nightmare was about a clown or a doll. Maybe something came out of the shadowy closet or from under the bed to eat your toes.

These are things small children are afraid of, but sometimes the fears stick with us and get locked in a room that we never want to visit. I used to think the nightmare room was just in my head, and I would go there often because that's the kind of adult I grew up to be. Then I had to spend two nights in a real nightmare room.

The nightmare room is real, folks. Come with me and I will show you.

#

I was three or four when I had the dream about the spider. Say whatever you want about not remembering things from such an early age and I will disagree. I have memories older than this nightmare. Some things we recall in snapshots and fragments, but I remember this dream like it was a film clip playing in the corner of the computer screen as I write this.

I was on the floor, reaching beneath my bed for an open roll of Lifesavers that I had lost shortly after Christmas. As my small fingers stretched to reach the candy, a large translucent spider crawled to my hand and bit me. Its glistening fangs pierced the skin of my hand as I looked into its many-orbed eyes, and I screamed. The Lifesavers rolled toward the wall as I pulled myself out from under the bed. I grasped my hand and howled for my mommy.

This is the point where I would probably wake up now, if I had this dream as an adult. Ask my wife. I often wake up screaming due to some mental misadventure during the middle of the night. I tend to remember these final images more than any other dreams. It is how my brain works.

I did not wake up after being bitten by the dream-arachnid. I did not wake up when my dream-self screamed for comfort. I did not wake up as I dreamt that a man in black pants and a purple jacket appeared in my room at the same time as my mom. He had dark hair, deep-set eyes, a drooping mustache, and golden teeth. The spider that bit me crawled out from under the bed, up his leg and into his coat pocket. As my mom reached for me, he stepped closer and placed his hand on my head.

"No. He's mine," the man said. His voice stopped my mom cold. I stood up, still holding my swelling hand, and walked with him into and through the wall.

Perhaps then I awoke. It's possible I remained asleep and merely rolled over, adjusting my Sesame Street quilt around my body as I tossed and turned. The dream stayed with me, although I don't remember telling anyone about it. Now that I think about it, I don't know if I've ever talked about this nightmare that has implanted itself into my memory for more than thirty years.

This must make us friends because I want to hear

about your nightmares, too.

#

If I wanted any sleep that night about halfway through our visit to my father-in-law's home, I would only get it by sleeping on the twin bed in the second downstairs bedroom instead of the double bed in the guestroom with my wife. Our son hasn't been sleeping well and the double bed just wasn't big enough for the three of us. So, I made the sacrifice and went to the room next door.

My stepmother-in-law must have used every possible cliché of childhood phobias to decorate the room. On one wall is a massive, round mirror: a perfect portal for any goblin royalty to reach through and steal away with an unaware child. Opposing the mirror is a deep closet that has nothing in it but shadows and dread. Filled with boxes, the closet might be less sinister. Fill it with clothes and it would only become a storage unit for malevolent apparitions.

The hall-facing wall is no better. On the other side of the wall is the opposing guest room. This shouldn't be a problem, except that instead of a solid wall separating the two rooms there is a shuttered rectangle of space. Light from the other room seeps in as if there's a force trying to break through and haul you up by hooks and chains. The light isn't the worst part. Like a good horror movie, the sounds of things unseen are much more frightening. This passage allows easy access to all noises from slumbering sighs to midnight moans. Yet there is just enough slatted wood in the way to make voices unintelligible. The person or persons on the other side of the wall could be cooing each other back to sleep or plotting your demise.

A mirror, a closet, a portal to another room: these would be enough to kickstart one's sense of impending doom. But like a TV pitchman, I have more.

You can't have a true nightmare room without a bed that sits a foot off the ground. Ample room for whatever boogeymen were unable to use the closet to crawl into your nightmares. During the day, the height of the bed makes it easy to clear out any dust bunnies or creepy crawlies—spiders, of course I'm thinking of spiders—that might be hiding under there. At night … at night, it doesn't matter if the accumulation of debris has been cleared and there is proof no multi-legged creatures that only God loves live under there. At night, it just means that whatever lives beneath the bed has less clutter to get through before reaching up and grabbing your foot or your hand and pulling you down into Hell.

Have you had enough, or do you want to hear about the three-foot-tall teddy bear that lives on the bed when no one is sleeping in it? Or the collection of dolls, including two sizes of Raggedy Ann and Andy dolls, staring down from a shelf above the bed?

I spent two nights in the nightmare room, "dreaming dreams no mortal ever dared to dream before," as Poe said. In many ways, I am always in the nightmare room, and that is where we now meet.

#

This book is a mirror, revealing the faces of fear and hope we see every day. This book is a darkened closet and the space beneath the bed; it is a place where monsters live and wait for that moment when your eyes are about to close, when you are vulnerable and unable to defend yourself. It is a collection of dolls ready to jump off the shelf and show you new ways to play "house."

This is a portal to another room. One that looks much like the room you are in now, but darker. It's as welcoming as grandma's house and as dangerous as grandma's attic.

You may not share all the same nightmares that I have, but there is something for you here. There are ghosts and divorces, acts of love and acts of violence. There is poetry, which I know scares some of you, and one piece of scholarship, which probably scares even more of you.

All I ask is that you follow me into the nightmare room and I will do my best to make sure you make it out with all of your fingers and toes. I can't promise much more than that.

#

For the record, I'm not afraid of spiders.

August 11, 2016
Moscow, Idaho

Hemingway at Work

"Hemingway at Work" is a fun piece that I wrote in one sitting. I was having one of those days when I needed to write something new to get away from a work in progress but had no idea what I wanted to write. I used an old trick and grabbed a random book off the shelf, opened to a random page, and with my eyes closed pointed to a sentence. That sentence became the first line of this story. You should try it if you are ever stuck for an idea.

This story has no scientific basis other than that there are weird viruses out there that can do some horrible shit. I made one up to suit my story and named it after another writer. "Myrbo," for those wondering, means plague or contagion in Italian, depending on what internet translation site you use.

You don't know me, but I know you. I'm an employee. That's why I won't sign my name to this letter. That would put my job at risk. You have to know how far you can go. I'm still figuring that out. What I know is that I still need this job. If I signed this, human resources would be on me faster than you earn a dollar.

For now, you will just have to live without knowing who I am. I'm sure I'll slip up somewhere and give myself away. Or I could lie and plant details to make you think I'm someone else. I could tell you the age of the prostitute you spent the night with on your last business trip to London, but since you don't even know exactly how old he was, that wouldn't help.

I know things about you and this company that an employee in my position shouldn't know. It disgusts me. Don't get angry yet. You'll burst a vein before we even get to the good stuff.

And don't for a second think this is blackmail. Other than my job, you have nothing I want. You can't properly bribe me since you don't know who I am.

Enough about me. Let's talk some more about you. I have a feeling you aren't convinced of my knowledge. Let's talk about March 27, 1995. Best day ever, right? How many people died that day? Seven? Early reports rumored deaths in the dozens, but from my research only seven people, including two children, actually died from your actions that day. Thousands more have died because of that Tuesday, but still, only seven.

Do you remember their names? Did you ever know them? Brad Irby is surely familiar. He's the one who sued you in 1993. Cost you a year of your life. A year well-spent, was it? Concocting revenge plots. Scenarios to get back at him and his wife for nearly ruining your life.

Did you have to infect his daughter, too? Or the Forshams next door? They'd only been married for six months. Did you know that? No, I think not. You are too narrow-minded a monster to consider the collateral damage. You shoot mosquitoes with bazookas.

One would think that with your mind, one would think you would have considered that the bacteria would spread and somehow reach the other two apartments on Irby's floor. One would think you would have found a way to block the vents to seal in your manufactured disease instead of letting it get to the two old women sharing the apartment above the Irbys. You are lucky you didn't breathe in the last cloud of germs and die that day, too. No, it was a paperboy who breathed his last after you'd left.

How many other families have you destroyed in the twenty years since then? Even I don't know all of them. All those civilians in Syria who breathed in your custom-made biological weapons. Do you think I would have taken this job if I knew what kind of man you were?

I might have, at that. I have a family and they need fed. My wife, our two-and-a-half children, dog, and cat all need food and shelter. This job, working for you, provides those necessities. And it makes me want to vomit.

One thing I have never figured out about Brad Irby. How did you not get caught? And when it came time to sign your government contracts, why weren't the connections made between your simple bacteria and the nearly undetectable viruses used to wipe out entire villages on the other side of the world? I know you were questioned regarding the Irby massacre but skated away without a charge.

Did you learn how to grease the right palms then, or had you been doing that before? You couldn't put enough grease in Brad Irby's hand to shut him up, so you filled his three-bedroom flat like a concentration camp shower house and murdered seven people.

And got away with it.

Does all of your money help you sleep at night? Your wife must not be helping much or you wouldn't have to sleep with boys in other countries. Did that start before you killed Irby, too? I know it's not a new thing for you. Didn't the esteemed Senator from Georgia once mention an incident during his second stag party? Something about you being disappointed in the cake? Hoping it would be a different flavor than twenty-year-old buxom blonde? Sadly, your proclivities aren't illegal in some of the countries in which you practice. So, I must be satisfied with what I can prove to be illegal in this country. As if murder weren't enough.

I wish I could go back and ask Brad Irby what he really knew. He only sued you for wrongful termination—and what a phrase that is—but why was that enough to kill him? He, his wife, and his daughter were dead long before February 18, 2004, so it couldn't have been that.

I was with the company seven years by then, well above entry-level. If the Army recruiters were as good as yours, I would have suited up in camouflage right out of high school. I could have ended up working for you anyway, as it turns out. No one tried to tell me not to work for you.

That was a rough year. The company made $16 billion off the war, and I started to pay for selling my soul. Three people I supervised, two who were hired at the same time as I was, died during experiments.

There. That should narrow it down from two thousand employees to fifty. I mean forty-eight.

I'm starting to wonder if it even matters who I am anymore. I hang my head in shame when I go home every day. My wife sees it. My kids see it. But Daddy must provide. We might have to give up the dog. I can't blackmail you into restoring my pride.

It's been ten years since Brent, Lisa, and Roger died in the basement. Collateral damage. Zigged when they should have zagged. They panicked. All those damn training videos teaching us to stay calm, take shallow breaths, and get to the showers as fast as possible. Not them. The vial broke, and Roger gulped in air and screamed. He was dead before anyone else knew he'd dropped anything. Scared Lisa into an asthma attack, which could have saved her. Shallow breathing, right? But no. When my kid breaks his arm, I'm grateful for our health coverage. Our great insurance paid for the fast-acting inhaler Lisa used to get her lungs full of tainted oxygen. Brent, the idiot, had his heart in the right place. He ran to save Lisa, to perform CPR. He breathed in her death as he tried to breathe life back into her.

I'm one of the certified safety members, too. I should have tried to help. I ran. I saw Roger hit the floor and bolted. I could have died a hero to my co-workers and nameless to the rest of the world. My family would have been taken care of. That's part of the deal. Dying at work pays off quadruple.

I hear Brent's wife lives in Maui now.

Quitting, which I should have done then, doesn't pay shit. I thought we were going to save the world through science, not kill it off in waves of sickness. I wanted to cure diseases, not create new plagues.

And there you sat, one branch churning out trendy viruses and another making money off vaccines. No one—no one who lived long enough to say so, anyway—bothered to ask where all these new flu strains were coming from. Everyone just accepted them as the usual mutations. As long as the casualties were mostly foreign, few seemed to care.

How is Shirley, anyway? That's her name, right? How could you let your own daughter spend two years in South America fighting diseases you created? Wouldn't the media love to know that Sister Margaret Lourdes was actually Shirley Myrbo, only daughter of pharmaceuticals pioneer Paul Myrbo? The Church is great at burying the backgrounds of some of its missionaries, but enough digging will always bring the bones to light. I'm looking at the *Newsweek* photograph of her funeral. I recognized the deep-set eyes in her mugshot from the photograph you keep on your desk. Your friend from Georgia attended the service, along with a few other important people. All to honor someone who died trying to save strangers.

You know who wasn't there? You. You could have gotten away with it. Her group was using your vaccines and medicines, after all. It's an adequate cover story, if anyone had asked. If they had, would you have been crying enough to give yourself away? I have my doubts.

Shirley died not long after Lisa, Brent, and Roger. That's when I started to realize just how evil you are. You didn't have anyone to fire because of their accident. They were dead. Everyone else followed protocol and ran. I have a feeling you wrote that policy. Let those who make a mistake pay for it. Save your own ass. I know you've put in plenty of overtime to get where you are.

But so have I. I have the certificate above my desk to show for it. It says "Employee of the Year," but it really should say "Most Overtime Hours without Dying." I probably spend more time in my office than you do in yours. No junkets with congressmen to Thailand for me. It shouldn't surprise you that I've created a few deadly bugs of my own. Not for public consumption, of course. And, since I'm not an evil bastard like you, I have the cures to all of them.

My favorite one—I call it Hemingway—lives on paper. It's communicated by touch only. It's one hundred percent non-contagious. You can only get it by direct contact with the virus. After about four hours of exposure to room temperature air, Hemingway, and the paper it lives on, begins to disintegrate, leaving nothing but a pile of flakes.

By now, you should be sweating and your pulse will be heightened. I know, you thought it was just because this letter was pissing you off. Alas, no. That's Hemingway at work. I won't be writing much more because your vision is about to get blurry. You'll have about ten minutes before your throat seizes and you can't speak.

One last thing. Once inside your body, the Hemingway virus will only live long enough to kill you. Based on rodent testing, that's between thirty-six and forty-eight hours. After that, it looks like the regular influenza virus. Once you die, it will appear as if you've had the flu and, at your age, couldn't fight it off. Calling in sick for that last trip down south made this perfect timing.

Goodbye, Mr. Myrbo.

Yours,

An Employee

Bury All Your Secrets in My Skin

I had set out to write a story in which no one died. In that regard, "Bury All Your Secrets in My Skin" is a failure. But what a beautiful failure it became.

This is one of the newer stories collected here and is now among my favorites. I'm still learning how to write strong women (as many male writers are), but Corrie feels real to me. Her situation is simultaneously extraordinary and all too normal and I had a blast writing her.

There are some musical references in this piece, as I am highly influenced by whatever I happen to be listening to when I write. The soundtrack for this story is "Snuff" by Slipknot and the Allman Brothers' "Midnight Rider."

After her sixteenth birthday, a much older friend of Corrie's father gave her her first broken heart. He said he loved her as the black ink traced a cracked ventricle just above her left breast. He kissed her when the outline was complete and deflowered her on the sofa before changing the ink from black to red. The motor of his tattoo gun — a prison special put together from a guitar string, a ball point pen, and the motor from a broken Dremel drill — smoked, and Corrie focused on the tendrils of yellowish smoke instead of on the throbbing pain on her chest. If there was pain below, she didn't notice. He told her losing her virginity wouldn't hurt as much as getting her first tattoo, so she might as well do both at the same time. He didn't so much force himself on Corrie as highly suggest that she did not have an option. She gave in, and didn't cry or produce more than a whimper as he entered her.

She kept her head turned away, watching the tattoo gun as it rested, instead of looking into his reddening face. Her lungs filled with his sour breath, and the distant taste of mint made her want to vomit. Her father's friend continued breathing heavily as he prepared his makeshift tattoo gun for the next round. "I'm finished," he said, "so let's finish you." He had not been wearing a shirt during the previous five minutes, so he had only to pull his pants back up. He and the gun seemed to struggle, but Corrie believed they would both fulfill their tasks. The tiny motor whirred to life, ready to vibrate the guitar string that would push the red ink into her skin forever. Forever was much longer than the time it took for Corrie to give herself to her father's friend. Her heart, the old one beating just beneath the new one, would take forever to heal, she'd convinced herself.

Her father's friend, Gary, looked like an older version of the boy who had broken her real heart, another idea that, like the time she would take to heal, Corrie had needed to convince herself of. He—Gary, not the high school boy Corrie hoped was hurting just as much as she was—told her all love hurt. He told her every tattoo on his body was because of love. He must love the Tasmanian Devil an awful lot, Corrie thought, and had to fight for control of the giggles or she might move and Gary would mess up her ink. She closed her eyes and looked for the face of the boy who left her alone at the Homecoming dance. Less than a second and his face floated behind her eyes. She allowed herself to sink into it. She imagined her body being tattooed on his face just as she allowed Gary to give her a new heart. She wanted to stretch and pull the boy into her. Not in the same way she had let Gary into her, but in a way that she could absorb the boy's entirety: body, mind, spirit — if such a thing existed. And then he would be hers, forever.

"We're done, sugar," Gary said and then softly blew on the tortured skin. He gently wiped drops of blood from her breast and lingered over her sheet-covered nipple. She opened her eyes to see him, a friend of her father's, leaning in to kiss her. She turned her head and Gary's lips landed on her neck. She scooched away from him, careful not to bump the sensitive skin of her chest, and grabbed the button-up shirt she had worn earlier that night.

"Thank you," she said, adjusting her skirt and gathering her panties, trying to remember if Gary's bathroom was down the hall to the left or upstairs. When she had visited Gary's house as a child with her father, the bathroom had been off the living room, just like in the trailer she lived in three spots down. But that had been ten years and a different town ago, before Corrie knew what *ovaries* were and what *ovarian cancer* meant.

Corrie's face pulled into a momentary frown as she recalled the needles and tubes going into and coming out of her mother. Her memory flooded her mouth with the gooey taste of the Tootsie Rolls her father had decided were the best comfort food available and the wafting scent of the lilacs that filled the hospital room. The old taste and scents mixed with the mint residue from Gary's breath, and Corrie again stifled the urge to vomit. Her chest burned, and she imagined the flesh around her tattoo rippling.

Instead of the bathroom, Corrie found the kitchen. The counter, twice the length of the counter she used to sit on in Gary's old trailer as she listened to her mother and Gary's wife Dawn talk about their other neighbors in the trailer park, was covered in plastic baggies. Half of the baggies lay flat on the counter empty, their open mouths waiting to be filled. Crumbled leaves and three green bricks she recognized as marijuana took up the rest of the table. Her heart—the real one—pounded as she considered stealing a baggie or maybe asking Gary for a sample. She trembled at the thought of what Gary would ask for in return. Her dad had rolling paper, she knew, but he claimed they were for cigarettes. Corrie knew the truth, but didn't want to ask him to borrow his Zig-Zags. She hadn't seen him in three days, anyway.

"Hey, girl, you find that bathroom yet?" Gary said from the living room.

"Got turned around, but I found my way," she lied.

"Don't touch anything if you're in the kitchen," he said, and she heard him standing. His weight, which less than an hour before seemed like a large helium balloon, shook the house as he walked toward where she stood. Her chest throbbed with each pump of blood from her heart and every breath in her lungs. She gave herself so easily to him, knocked on his door and asked him to tattoo her, not to help her forget Trevor, the boy who invited her to Homecoming then forgot about her.

Trevor, in all his senior class treasurer and football wide receiver glory, loomed before her. Corrie pictured him running on the football field as he she was getting her tattoo and giving up her virginity. She could hear his jock friends laughing, joking about how Trevor didn't need motherless and desperate Corrie to score when he could be scoring touchdowns Friday night and with cheerleaders on Saturday.

"I told you not to touch anything," Gary said.

Corrie blinked, coming back to herself, and saw baggies of weed clutched in her hands.

"I said, I told you not to touch anything," Gary said. "What do you think you're doing, sugar?"

Corrie willed herself to let go of the bags, but instead she gripped them tighter, piercing the plastic with her fingernails. A new vision of Trevor came to her: not absorbing him, but tearing him apart. She threw her hands in front of her, screaming as the sudden extension of her arms pulled away the gauze covering the damaged skin of her left breast. Her scream slowed Gary before he reached Corrie.

"Quiet down, girl," Gary said. "You'll bring the neighbors over and we don't want that."

Corrie stopped her screaming, but her new heart pulsed pain through her torso as her old heart pumped blood through her body. Her right hand relinquished its grip on the marijuana baggie, and she pressed the hand to her chest. Despite the pain, the tenderness of her skin surprised her. She had expected the tattoo to toughen her, not to make her more vulnerable. She pulled her hand away, seeing splotches of red that could have been blood or excess ink.

As she pondered her hand and the pain, Gary closed in, his bulk becoming light again as he silently approached Corrie. She looked up just before Gary's fist connected with her temple.

Corrie didn't see stars; she saw hearts like her own: red and black, breaking down the middle as they floated around her head. A second eruption of broken hearts filled her vision when her head slammed against the kitchen floor.

#

"Austin, it's me, Gary," Corrie heard through the pounding in her head. She was on the couch again, covered to her chin with a clean sheet. An ice pack melted on her head, tendrils of condensation trickling into her closed eyes and open mouth.

"No, she's not fucking OK." Gary's voice became louder, matching the aching of her temples. Corrie opened her eyes and didn't see Gary. She listened and heard the creaking of the kitchen floor, the boards taking the brunt of Gary's weight. She shook her head, causing a spike of pain to tear through her skull, but it soon faded. She reached up and felt the lump on the side of her head and winced. She checked herself for any other bumps or cuts, and one finger slid lightly across the gauze covering her tattoo. *I am still bleeding*, she thought. *I need to get out of here.*

"No, fuck you, Austin. You come and get her. I can't leave. I'm in the middle of packing, and your little bitch almost ruined it."

The voice on the other end of the line was Corrie's dad, she realized. She knew her dad and Gary had a long history, so he wouldn't be as surprised to see the spread in Gary's kitchen as she had been. He might be more surprised to find out how she ended up unconscious and what had gone on just prior to Gary cold-cocking her. She'd never intended to tell him, but he would find out soon enough.

"Yes…Yes… No. Sounds like she's waking up. You just get your ass over here." Corrie jumped at the sound of Gary slamming the phone back onto its cradle. Her last phone call, a teenager's call to her father, had concluded with her angrily pressing the END button on her cellphone.

"Well, look who woke back up," Gary said from the hallway. "You just about got yourself in worse condition than you are. If somebody'd come over to ask what the screaming was about, shit, who knows what might have happened."

He approached her—stalked her, she thought—with his large arms swaying at his sides. Corrie noticed he'd finally put a shirt on, a concert T-shirt with a picture of a red plastic cup on it. She scrunched herself up into one end of the couch, as far away from him as she could get. He sat at the other end, turned so half his body faced her.

"Your daddy is on his way to get you. Seems he didn't know you were coming here or where you were at all." He scratched his chin and Corrie saw spots of red and black ink on his fingers.

If those fingers come near me again, I'll bite them off, she thought.

"Are you listening? I told him what happened. That you came over because you got some jackass to give you a tattoo and you wanted me to look at it to make sure it was done right. You were in the bathroom when you passed out from the pain and because you hadn't eaten anything today, and then you bashed your head into the sink.

"And you'd better fucking remember it just like that," Gary said.

Corrie pulled her legs closer to her body, pulling the sheet at the same time, trying to fight off the chill she got from Gary's words. Her gut clenched and she felt like she could take another punch, but that didn't mean she wanted to. She couldn't close her eyes and retreat to the place in her mind where Trevor had not stood her up. She feared Gary would try to shift his position on the couch closer to hers if she stopped looking at him. She couldn't go to the time when her mom pushed her on the swings while her dad played his guitar and drank beer with his friends, either. Gary was there, before both men got sent away and before her mom died. *I'm stuck here. He won't let me leave.*

As Corrie thought of the horrors that awaited her— running drugs, being beaten and raped, and eventually killed —if she were left in Gary's house, she heard the off-kilter rumble of her dad's Mustang. The 1970 fastback had holes in the exhaust that never would have been there if her dad had cared about anything since her mom died. He'd made a joke once that he'd give the car to her first boyfriend, and if he could fix it, he'd let the boy keep dating her. She planned to tell Trevor that story during the dance, but that didn't happen, and now here she was. Her dad must not have been too far away to get to Gary's house so soon, but Corrie had no idea how long she'd been blacked out. He could have been down the street or across town at Palm Cheyenne, the cemetery Corrie hadn't visited herself in more than a year.

The car stopped, and Corrie caught the last notes of The Allman Brothers "Midnight Rider" before her dad turned off the Mustang. *Somebody's in trouble*, she thought.

Austin, her dad, only listened to "Midnight Rider" when he was angry. Corrie remembered first hearing the song the night before the cops took Austin to jail when she was six and again the night after her mom died when Corrie was ten and her mouth was full of melting Tootsie Rolls.

Austin pounded on the door. "Open the door, asshole," he yelled. "If you so much as looked at her funny, I'll break your fat neck."

As Gary stood to answer, he winked at Corrie and put one of his sausage fingers to his lips, reminding her to not change the story he had provided. "Man, I've been registered since the Becker girl ratted me out, so don't talk shit before you even get in the door," Gary said, opening the door. Austin pushed his shoulder into the door and knocked Gary's obese body to the floor.

"Corrie, baby, you OK?" Austin asked when he saw her on the couch. She nodded, first looking her dad in the eyes, then just over his shoulder. Her eyes widened and she wanted to scream, but Gary brought the butt of a gun down on Austin's head before she could warn him.

"Motherfucker knock me down in my house," Gary said. "You hear him call me a molester? Fucker should've known what you came here for."

He bent down, patting Austin around the waist and ankles, searching for weapons. Corrie's hands gripped the sheet just as they had when she tore into the baggies. She watched Austin take shallow breaths and worried for him.

The traumatized skin over her heart convulsed, and her blood pulsed through her veins like lava. She stood, ripped open her shirt, and tore the gauze off her tattoo. The heart had grown, covering almost her entire breast, and the dark outline had sprouted, sending thorned branches across her chest and up her neck.

The black branches squirmed on her skin as if they were trying to break free from her body. She saw new pinpoints of blood emerge where the tips of thorns formed.

"Gary," she said. "Something's wrong."

"Fucking right, something's…" Gary stopped speaking as he looked up at Corrie. His mouth dropped open and the gun he held clanked to the floor. "What the fuck?"

Sharp points pushed through Corrie's skin, surrounding the ink heart in blood. Her flesh seared around the thorns. Corrie expected to smell rancid smoke or cooking flesh, but instead her nose filled with the perfume of lilacs.

Her mother's favorite.

The ink branches tore themselves from Corrie's chest and shot toward Gary. As they sped toward him, they thickened, and the thorns sharpened. Corrie thought that maybe just the ends would touch Gary, try to scare him, but instead four of the thickest branches wrapped around his throat. The thorns dug into his skin, and blood brighter than the ink Gary had used to give Corrie her broken heart jetted from his throat. Darker blood, almost the color of the branches squeezing the life from Gary, seeped beneath the branches, soaking the cowboy band and their plastic cup on his shirt.

A wayward branch slithered its way toward Austin, gliding through his hair. It stopped at the wound Gary had left on Austin's head, darted into the wound, and came up with a drop of blood dangling from the tip. Corrie heard a slurping sound and watched as the drop of her father's blood disappeared into the branch.

The branch turned back toward her father. "No," she said and the branch retreated.

Gary's eyes had remained on Corrie even as they bulged out of their sockets. She turned away, and the branches let go. They shrank and burrowed back into Corrie's skin, leaving faint trails of blood. Once she felt the branches were back inside her, she wiped herself with the sheet. When she looked at her exposed breast, the heart had returned to its original size but had changed.

She stepped over Gary and knelt beside her father.

"Dad," she whispered, but he did not answer. His breathing had steadied and she did her best to check for a pulse. Satisfied that he would live, she spoke to him again. "Dad. I have to go. You'll need to clean up here, but I know you can. I need to take care of something else."

As she left her father behind in Gary's house, she looked at her tattoo again, not entirely covered by her ruined shirt. The crack Gary had embedded into her flesh was no longer there; her once-broken heart had healed.

Nutjob

I met Michelle Kilmer at Crypticon Seattle in 2014. She was mutual Facebook friends with writer/editor Kriscinda Lee Everitt and I made it a point to contact Michelle via the platform. As it so happened, I ran into Michelle and her twin sister Becky Hansen in the elevator on the first day. Elevator meetings like that are awkward and this was no exception. Friendship grew and I not only purchased Michelle's solo novel When the Dead *but also the collection she co-wrote with Becky* The Spread. *After the convention, Michelle and I stayed in contact and I pitched her the idea that became* Give: An Anthology of Anatomical Entries. *We received stories from around the world based on the idea of hearing from organ donors. The entire collection is a delightful mix of dark humor, sci-fi, and horror.*

My story in the book is "Nutjob" and it is about exactly what you think it is about. Those sensitive orbs of tissue hanging between a man's legs. In many ways, it is also about the fears of being a new dad, which I had been for about a year when I wrote the story. It's closer in tone to the sci-fi of "Hemingway at Work" than traditional horror, but as many of you know, little kids can be creepy.

Keep your eyes open for more of Michelle Kilmer's kick-ass work under the name Michelle von Eschen and Take: An Anthology of Anatomical Entries Volume II *coming soon.*

Parker saw them everywhere: red-haired, blue-eyed monsters. Once, a girl of maybe three walked right up to him, glaring at him with an ocean of hate in her eyes, and said, "Daddy." He reached down to pat her on the head, but stopped short. Instead, he scratched himself, feeling the place where the matched set he was born with was now incomplete. It had been that way for four years.

A stupid credit card he never should have signed up for, student loans coming due, and a pressing need to eat every day forced Parker into the sperm donation office. He'd donated plasma before, but that had become a hassle. You had to go twice a week to make any real money and Parker often missed a day and had to cycle back to the beginning. He could make, he was told, as much in one session donating sperm as he could in a month of plasma donations. Parker had nowhere else to be that day, so the sign on the door did not turn him away.

NOTICE:
FIRST TIME DONORS
ALLOW FOR 6-8 HOURS
SCREENING AND PROCESSING

He expected to be looked at like a pervert—movies taught him that this sort of place was perfect for pervs looking to get paid just to jerk off—but the matronly woman at the counter barely looked up as she handed him a clipboard loaded with forms.

"Fill these out and don't lie," she said. "We'll know if you do."

Parker didn't say anything. He took out the pen he always carried (the thought of using a pen held by who-knows-how-many paid masturbators gave Parker the creeps), and sat in the plain white plastic chair farthest from the front desk. Everything seemed to be made out of the same hard white plastic, even the clipboard on Parker's lap. He filled out the form, not unlike the form he filled the first time he donated plasma, but noticed that the section for emergency contacts was blocked off, seeming to make that information more important. Parker had but one word for that section: NONE. He wrote the same word on the line following "Next of Kin" and "Current Dependents." He signed and dated the last line, stood up, walked over to the desk and handed back the clipboard. He gave his "you're welcome" without hearing a "thank you" from the receptionist and headed back to his seat. The waiting room remained empty.

"Mr. Parker," an authoritative voice said before his ass reached plastic. "This way." A woman, with similar, but softer features than the receptionist, beckoned to him from a glass door. Parker tried to admire her figure, you know, to get in the mood, but the shapeless shift—white like everything else —hid whatever curves she had from him. She led Parker down a spotless hall and through another door that Parker didn't even see until the woman opened it.

"Wait here, please," she said and closed the door behind her. The room contained nothing but another chair like the one in the waiting room. The walls, the floor, and the ceiling were all the sterile white that Parker was not getting used to.

He twitched and scratched and waited. His balls itched the worst but he tried not to scratch there. He knew there were probably hidden cameras and he didn't want to seem too eager. After what seemed like an hour, but was only about five minutes, a voice spoke from one of the walls.

"Welcome, Mr. Parker. We're happy you have chosen to visit us." A red square appeared on the wall near where Parker thought the voice emanated. "Please place your hand on the red square, palm down."

The intrusion of color into the blank world didn't so much throw Parker for a loop as it attracted him. He stepped closer to the wall and put out his hand. Immediately, he felt tiny pinpricks on his fingers.

"Thank you. The blood test will determine your suitability as a donor."

"How long will that take?" Parker asked, although he could not be sure he was speaking to an actual person.

"Test complete.

"Mr. Parker, we'd like to offer you an enhanced donation option. For a significant upfront payment and subsequent monthly payments, we would ask that you donate more than just sperm."

"How much?" Not *what do you want* but *how much*. Was Parker truly that desperate? No, but he was curious enough to keep his options open.

The red square turned green and some black type appeared within it. The big number was enough to pay off his student loans. With the small number, he could pay off his credit card in less than a year and maybe even afford his own apartment. "Where do I sign?"

"You already have, Mr. Parker."

The white room went black and Parker felt a small stab in his neck. Before he lost consciousness, he felt his shoes being removed and his pants being pulled down.

He drifted in and out of consciousness, at one point telling a disembodied face that he was a redhead and needed more anesthesia. A moment later, he thought he heard someone say something about testicles and how he would only need one. He didn't think too much about it. Those big numbers consumed his thoughts and he returned to the darkness.

\#

Parker didn't wake up in his own bed because he didn't have a bed of his own. He woke, sore in a particularly sensitive area, on a bench in the park where a little girl would call him Daddy not quite four years later. In his right pocket was a deposit receipt with more zeroes than any other number. In his left pocket, the side that hurt the most, Parker found a roll of twenties, a note with the phone number of a local real estate agent, and a bank account number. At the bottom the note was signed:

> Thank you for your kind donation.
> -Ilene

Parker felt like a free man, if not a whole one, when the account and the real estate agent checked out. For a year, he lived within his new means and with no debt hanging over his head. The urge to return to the donation center caught him off guard, but going back did not seem necessary. His new account was always replenished on the first day of the month and he never asked questions. Sometimes, he had to scratch himself more than average, but even that was only a minor inconvenience. Instead of going back to the office where he had his left testicle removed—donated to whatever unknown cause the voices behind the white walls served—he went back to the park where he woke up that day.

He sat on the bench—*his* bench—and zoned out. He was glancing toward the twisty slide when he saw a little boy with copper on his head and the summer sky in his eyes. The boy wore black shorts, a Batman shirt and a goofy lopsided smile, and Parker thought he recognized him.

He stood up, hoping to see someone chasing after the small boy who could barely walk, but saw no one nearby. Thinking the boy was lost and separated from his parents, Parker approached, but as he closed in, he remembered where he had seen the boy before.

It's me. That boy is me. Parker, with no family left alive, had the image imprinted on his heart: him, barely one, showing off his Batman shirt and his crooked, goofy smile. His scrotum tightened, easier now than a year ago without the extra testicle, and he shivered in the heat.

And then he ran.

A year later, he was back at the park. He didn't see the boy in the Batman shirt, but he did see a trio of copper-headed toddlers sitting on his bench. He didn't stay long enough to see their faces, to see if their eyes were blue.

On the third anniversary of waking up on the bench, Parker tried to stay away, but he couldn't help himself. His scrotum itched and his one remaining ball wanted to be better friends with gravity, pulling him body and soul to the ground. Like the extra space in his scrotum, the bench and the park were empty. He sat down and stared at the twisty slide for an hour before leaving. As he walked through the parking lot, a black mini-van cruised by him. The van was full of little redheads.

He did not see the driver.

For the next year, he saw them everywhere: all with steel-blue eyes and hair like polished copper. A glint of pale skin and a few freckles would flash by in a car mirror while Parker waited for a bus. He would see a pair of eyes staring at him from across a restaurant and he would stare back, like looking into the sky. He never saw any adult around these children who all looked like him. He imagined a white wall between each child and the child's guardian, a wall so clean no one could see it, but so solid that Parker's own eyes couldn't penetrate it.

Parker's fourth visit to the park was the first time one of the children spoke to him. Just that one word—Daddy—and Parker wanted to put his hand on her head, but his scrotum retracted, reminding him of the day he went to donate sperm. Parker dropped to his knees and asked the only question he could think of.

"Where's your mommy?"

The girl smiled and pointed to the sky. Parker slumped, making him appear shorter than the girl, and looked to where her small finger aimed. He saw an army of three-year-old redheads, all taller than him from his submissive position, swarming toward him. He assumed they all had blue eyes, but he didn't notice. His own eyes focused instead on the mass of sharp white teeth gnashing toward his softest parts.

An Appointment with the Knifeman

I won't tell you the name of the door-to-door kitchen knife sales company I tried to get a job with in Las Vegas when I started college. I didn't get the job, but I got a story out of it and in many ways, I got the better deal. I would have been a horrible salesman.

I love what is at play here. "An Appointment with the Knifeman" is one of those cat-and-mouse stories in which one character thinks he is the cat but really is the mouse. While the narrator in this story isn't afraid of anything, just imagine how frightening it must be to be a door-to-door salesman and never know who is on the other side of the door.

Salespeople must be as scared as the person hesitating about whether to open their door to a stranger.

This is one of the oldest stories in this collection. I include it because it is a fun piece inspired by "Tales from the Crypt" and hopefully gives you, friend, a glimpse into how this writer has grown.

My first appointment for the evening is at 7:30. Most clients do not schedule me this early. I tend to cater to the night crowd. I arrive at the home at 7:28. I've learned to be precise. Showing up too early can be horrific; showing up late can be deadly.

The trees and sidewalk are clear of leaves. Spots of frost have already begun to form on the lawn. The small home hovers over the front yard, a prison guard watching from his tower. I can see basement lights barely shining through the blacked out bottom windows. The rest of the house is dark. I hope the client has not forgotten about our appointment.

I climb out of my car and then walk up to the steps. At exactly 7:30, I ring the doorbell. The faint light, which had illuminated the lawn, goes out. A door inside the house slams. Anyone else might be tempted to ring the bell a second time. I resist; my client knows who is at the door because I ring only once. Just like opportunity.

The front door cracks open. I see half the face of tonight's client. It looks nothing like the drawings. Not all my clients are so lucky.

"Is that you, Mr. Cutter?" the half-face asks.

"None other, Mr. Harmer." Harmer. Sounds fake. But I'm one to talk, aren't I?

"Please," the door opens farther, "come in, Mr. Cutter. I heard of your impeccable timing but you've surprised me. I don't like surprises. I'll make an exception this time."

"I hope you'll make many more. You may be surprised and hopefully amazed at the quality of my product."

"We'll see about that."

"Yes, yes we will."

#

I walk back to my car to get my sample case. I never bring it with me to the door the first time. Some of my clients change their minds and do not wish to see me. Sometimes the client isn't home for whatever reason. So I leave the case in the car. I have a few other reasons but those reasons are mine to keep.

I return to the front door, case in hand. Mr. Harmer has turned on the living room light, allowing me to see where I should sit. I walk into the house then take my seat near the coffee table. My seat, of course, is the orange plastic chair. Stolen from some elementary school that Mr. Harmer can never forget. Mr. Harmer sits in the recliner at the other end of the table. I'm used to this sort of dominant/submissive treatment. Every client wants to be in charge. Every client thinks he is doing something new. The first to leave a note; the first to drive a panel van; the first to treat me like a child. I told Mr. Harmer that he was in for more surprises.

I heave my case onto the table. The table is just wide enough to accommodate the case. I open it, lifting one side and turning it toward Mr. Harmer. His eyes bulge, not an uncommon reaction.

The knives, each in their place, shine in the limited light. Each knife, from the three-inch paring knife to the 14-inch bread knife, is made of 420J stainless steel. Each of the knives offered by Cutterman Inc. is full tang constructed. Ginsu may slice tomatoes, Miracle blade might cut sheetrock, but Cutterman knives are guaranteed to slice through bone.

I'm very proud of these facts and I let Mr. Harmer know so. He scowls, grunts, and reaches for the cleaver. I gently lift the handle before Mr. Harmer can leave a fingerprint on it. Had I shifted the blade a half-inch to the left, Mr. Harmer would no longer have a thumb. I move a quarter-inch and nick his hand. His blood drips onto his table, not my knives. I don't think anyone would notice another drop of blood on Mr. Harmer's coffee table.

I know everything that touches the knives in my case. I know everyone who touches my knives.

I twirl the cleaver in my hand, slicing the air. I pull a black handkerchief from a pocket inside the case. I wipe the blade clean. Sparkling, as always.

"As you have just witnessed, Mr. Harmer, Cutterman Knives wipe clean. Even blood comes right off. That should be an especially enticing incentive to a man in your field."

"What do you know about it?" Mr. Harmer says. He springs out of his chair, leaning over the table. His snarl and sneer might scare seventeen-year-old girls, but it doesn't scare me.

"Please, Mr. Harmer. Sit back down. Do you think I would be here without knowing exactly who you are and what your business is?"

Mr. Harmer eases back into his chair. His body relaxes, but his eyes remain paranoid and watchful. I can tell he would rather be back in his basement. I replace the cleaver in its space and decide to go for the sell now.

"Mr. Harmer, let me show you the crown jewel of the Cutterman collection." I hold out a butcher knife. "As you can see, this knife is a whole four inches wide at the base of the blade. The length gives it that extra inch so many of our customers desire. The full-tang construction and 420J stainless steel make this the most durable knife of its type available anywhere."

Mr. Harmer's eyes melt into a look of lust, replacing paranoia. "Do you have any frozen steaks, Mr. Harmer?" I ask.

"I think so. Let me check the kitchen," Mr. Harmer answers. He stands up, eyes still on the butcher knife. He turns around when he reaches the kitchen doorway. I hear the refrigerator door open and the sounds of Mr. Harmer rummaging through his frozen foods.

"The thicker, the better, Mr. Harmer," I call out.

He comes back into the living room. "I don't seem to have any up here. Let me check the basement freezer. All my big stuff is down there." I wave my hand in assent. Mr. Harmer grins and that lustful gleam returns to his eyes. "I'll be just a second."

"I'll be right here," I say. Mr. Harmer heads for the door that leads down to the basement. I can picture that diffused light shining on the lawn again. The butcher knife resides firmly in my hand. I love the feel of this knife. It is our most popular and definitely my most favorite item.

Silently, I descend the steps into the basement, knife in hand. This demonstration will be better downstairs.

"I can't seem to find any thick steaks," Mr. Harmer yells. "I'm sorry."

"Don't be," I whisper into his ear. "This will do perfectly."

"What will do…" Mr. Harmer cannot finish his question with the knife buried in his chest.

"Can you feel how that extra length really does the job, Mr. Harmer?" I say to him. His arm goes behind him then back out. His hand is covered with blood. "Can you feel it?" I ask.

Mr. Harmer nods. His eyes close. No sale this time. Before our appointment is finished, I decide to take my commission out of Mr. Harmer.

Nail Shitter

I have been fortunate enough to work as a journalist off and on over the last decade. My specialty and preference has been for entertainment and music journalism. I love talking to bands whether they are megastars or on their first national tour. I even covered the week-long concert that is the Sturgis motorcycle rally in South Dakota.

The Almost Famous *experience prompted me to write this story of heavy metal tragedy as told by a journalist who had been accepted into the inner circle of one band. And when Kriscinda Lee Everitt put out her call for heavy metal-inspired stories for her journal* Despumation, *I knew "Nail Shitter" had found a home.*

We did have to include a note stating that this story has no relation to a defunct Florida metal band of the same name. It's true. I never heard of the band and I should have known that Nail Shitter was too good of a name to have not been taken. My bad.

Wait. Let me make sure this thing still works. If the tape breaks, I'm fucked. I think you'll hear Paul first, then me. Syd is on here, too, and that's what you and I both need to hear. Let me just rewind the tape and hear what I got.

Click.

"It's all lies. That asshole hasn't told the truth in five years."

"So ... the band isn't breaking up?"

"No, that's true. We are splitting up. I can't stand him. Has he ever told you where his dad was the night he was born? That's a lie, too. A good one, but shit, man, anyone could have made that up."

Click.

I could see the band members as they found their marks on the stage. Without the lights, only a handful of fans, those dedicated enough to arrive early, would know Nail Shitter was ready to play. The screams from the front row multiplied throughout the crowd until everyone at The House of Blues knew the show was about to begin.

"Nail Shitter! Nail Shitter! Nail Shitter!"

Bands should choose their names based on how the chant will sound. AC/DC doesn't chant well, so crowds yell for Angus. Nail Shitter doesn't chant well, either, but any excuse to say "shit" is always welcome.

From behind me, a rush of sweat and anticipation hit my back. It's a mob now. Individuality is lost and only the animal exists. Right now, it is a content animal, about to receive its meal. It's blood they want. Nail Shitter's audiences are cannibals and they would tear the band apart if they could. Like when you hold a newborn and you say, "You are so cute I could eat you."

Cannibals don't eat people because they hate them. They eat their own to absorb power and to express love, as twisted as that sounds.

I'm the only one out here who knows that this show is Nail Shitter's last gig.

Syd, Syd, Syd; you're up, brother. Back to the tape.

Click.

"Listen, Jed, it's not like I hate the other guys in the band. I don't. I don't even hate Paul. What I do hate is the band. I hate that we've become a joke. I hate that we've become something kids laugh at and then ignore. We haven't been around long enough to be ignored or laughed at."

Click.

Syd told me he didn't hate his band mates. I believed him. Thirty minutes later, Paul told me everything Syd said was a lie. Except the part about the band breaking up. It's hard to believe, but I think both of them were right.

Syd didn't hate Paul. He didn't hate Vikk or Steve. He loved them.

#

One light illuminated Steve Belzok. He stood behind the drum kit, arms in the air, enjoying the only moment the crowd would see him. Call it the drummer's curse, but very few of them get the face time of vocalists or lead guitarists. Few drummers are Keith Moon or Lars Ulrich. Or, god forbid, Phil Collins. Steve might take a swing at me if he thought I'd compared him to Phil Collins. I wouldn't mind, really.

A cymbal crash pulsated over the frantic crowd as Steve sat down. Before the echo dissipated, the remaining stage lights came to life and the other three members of Nail Shitter appeared to viewers beyond just the front row.

Vikk Hentser, lead guitar.

Paul D'Innecezo, vocals.

Syd Gust, bass.

Syd and Vikk hit a power chord as Steve tapped out the

opening beats of "Nail You Down," the band's latest single. The lights accentuated the white and black paint covering their faces. Paul's makeup was white and silver, not what is called "corpse paint" at all. He shines under the lights, more like Ace Frehley's Space Child, as he sang about nailing a woman to a wooden plank and having his way with her.

Nail you down,
So you can't get up.
Nail you down,
So just shut up.

No one ever claimed Nail Shitter were lyrical geniuses.

The House of Blues crowd sang along as best they could. Paul's vocals were typical of death metal: a low growl, not really singing at all. Thanks to Syd's backing vocals, the chorus was more intelligible.

Click.

"I fucking hate that song. 'Nail You Down.' What the fuck is that supposed to mean? Paul wrote the lyrics for it. God, I should have stopped him. I thought he was going to write one of those sex and Jesus songs. Holy Christ was I wrong."

"Yeah, but you wrote 'Barbed Wire Condom' and 'Acid Suppository,' among others. Paul's written less than a dozen songs in Nail Shitter's entire career. Why didn't you just take the title and run with it?"

"I'm not a fascist. People think I control every single move this band makes. Like I'm some demented mother who can't let her children decide things for themselves. Paul, Steve, and Vikk are big boys and they can make their own choices.

"Really, if I had complete control of this band, do you think half the shit the other guys have pulled would have happened?"

Click.

I hate doing it. I hate listening to the tapes of those final interviews. Syd sounds so defensive. I didn't want to think about Nail Shitter breaking up. Syd, though, he'd thought about it a lot. Turned out Paul was right. Syd did lie about the band breaking up. As the foremost—okay, only—journalist covering the band, I should have known.

Click.

"Remember the last time we were in Vegas?"

"Yes, Syd, I do. Two years ago, right? We went to see The Porch Swing close."

"I loved that store. I was pretty pissed off when it closed. I found an Australian copy of *Highway to Hell* there. Had my hands on *Dirty Deeds*, too, but let it go to some kid who looked like he needed it more than me."

"Did he have enough to buy it?"

"Nah, I bought it for him. Wish someone had bought me records when I was his age."

"How old was he?"

"Twelve, thirteen maybe. I didn't have shit then."

Click.

The Porch Swing couldn't make it. It lasted thirty years, a vinyl store that survived 8-tracks, cassettes, and CDs but couldn't beat digital downloading. Everything has its breaking point. A person can survive cancer and get into a car accident on the way home from the hospital. Shit happens.

I wore a "Nail Shitter happens" T-shirt until it fell off my back. They sold a million of those, on tour and through mail order. Sold a million more once Steve learned how to design a website.

I bought five of them. One signed by each member of the band and one just for wearing. Pieces of that one are hanging on my wall now, next to the gold record Syd gave me.

#

"If you didn't write about us, we never would have sold more than a thousand records. We wouldn't be here without you," Syd said during that final interview.

Denny Marx scowled all night at the press conference. He didn't want them to give me a record. He wanted to give mine to his grandma. Can you believe that? A death metal band giving a gold record to their manager's 80-year-old grandma?

"Can you believe this douche bag wanted us to give a record to his gramma instead of our pal Jed? Me and the boys like Jed better. We told Marx that if his gramma wanted a record, she'd have to come down to the studio and blow us all," Paul said to the few media people in attendance. I think *Rolling Stone* was there, some blond-haired intern wearing cowboy boots sent out on her first assignment.

I was drunker than Paul, not as drunk as Steve or Vikk, and Syd didn't drink at all. Ever. So the three empty vodka bottles found in his dressing room, yeah, those were a surprise. I'd known Syd for almost ten years. I never saw him drink. Not on his birthday, not on New Year's Eve, and not during any of Nail Shitter's six gold album press conferences.

And never, absolutely never, backstage.

Click.

"My dad was a drinker. He didn't start out that way, but who ever does? He didn't start drinking until he and my mom moved to England. I was born there. What a year. My parents move to England in May, 1976. I was born in June. We were back in Connecticut by July, '77. Before Halloween, my dad had left. After that, I saw him for a weekend every couple months. He would always be drunk, vodka usually but sometimes tequila, and tell me stories about rock concerts he went to. He told me he missed my birth because he was at the Sex Pistols show in Manchester that night. Fucking punk."

Click.

You can look it up. Sydney Gust, born June 4, 1976, to Eliza and Henry Gust at the Manchester Royal Infirmary just before 9 p.m. The hospital records indicate that Mr. Gust was not present but arrived early the next morning.

Wherever Henry Gust was that night, it was enough for him to spin a tale told to many sons and daughters: I was there. Really, there were only about forty people there, tops. Possibly as few as fifteen. Doesn't matter. Sydney believed his dad enough to get into music.

And he was good at it. Heavy metal doesn't get one a lot of musical cred, but Syd had a way.

After "Nail You Down" and a few other classic Nail Shitter tracks—"Satan's Placenta" and "Gangbang Sacrament" have always been my favorites—Syd is left alone on stage. He never speaks word. He didn't have to. Like John Paul Jones or Cliff Burton, Syd played bass like a classical musician. The ten-minute solo from "Methropolis," measures of Mozart mixed with Metallica, told his life story for anyone listening. He played three-chord punk riffs followed by Van Halen finger-tapping, all on the bass. The beast in front of him calmed, caught up in Syd's own majesty.

I hope no one forgets it.

Tomorrow, when Sydney's estate executors (I know them, and plan to use them myself, if I die before they do) start going through his house in L.A., they'll find all of his inspiration. Records—many bought from The Porch Swing—

take up more space than anything. The walls of three rooms are lined with shelves full of vinyl. Record store-style racks take up the centers of these rooms. Two rooms for rock in all its variations and one for everything else. Mostly classical and jazz.

I've been there.

I don't know that I will ever go back.

Click.

"The band is breaking up. Everyone knows it. It's time. After tonight, Nail Shitter is no more."

"C'mon, Syd, you're just kidding, right? You finally have a top ten hit, even without much radio play. Your first crop of fans bring their kids out to the shows, so you have a whole new generation to wow. Would it be possible for the band to continue without you? I hate asking you that because to me, and to millions of fans, you are Nail Shitter. There wouldn't be a band without you."

"There won't be a band without me. There won't be a band at all."

Click.

I wish Paul listened to Syd more often. He might have changed his mind about Syd's propensity for falsehoods.

#

He didn't look drunk. The medical examiner said his blood alcohol level was three times the legal limit. He didn't look stoned or high, but marijuana roaches were found in the room along with empty vials of cocaine.

Syd never drank. I guess we all assumed he'd left the drugs behind when he left his teens.

The toxin levels found in the blood of the other Nail Shitter members haven't been released yet.

Someone suggested I wait to write this until we have all the facts. That I shouldn't rush to get a story out if it might be inaccurate.

That it will seem like I'm just trying to make a fast dollar off someone else's tragedy.

Fuck that. Syd was my friend. To a lesser extent, so were Steve and Vikk. I don't think Paul ever liked me, but fuck him anyway.

Who needs a drink now? I do, I do.

Click.

"I'll see you tomorrow, Syd."
"Yeah, Jed, sure. See you tomorrow."

Click.

With ears still ringing from the show, no one heard the gunshots.

Steve and Vikk shared a dressing room at venues this size. You'd think House of Blues Las Vegas would be huge, but it holds only 800 people. Shows there sell out more often than not, especially big shows like Nail Shitter. A year from now, this show will be like that Sex Pistols gig in Manchester. Thousands of people will claim to have been there when only 800 could have been. Trust me, you'll hear it.

Dude, I was there! I was at the show when Syd blasted the rest of Nail Shitter and hung himself.

I totally heard the shots, man. That's why I always wait until I get kicked out. You never know what crazy shit will happen at a Nail Shitter show.

I saw somebody walk backstage with a rope during the set, bro! I bet it was the rope Syd used.

You get the point.

It is true that one never knew what might happen at a Nail Shitter show. Remember when Paul simulated sex with that goat at a Salt Lake City show? Of course you do. The band's big MTV moment hit the internet before the song reached the bridge. All for the prurient pleasure of their adoring fans and the Religious Right.

Everyone was there. I took the photos that clearly showed no actual penetration of the goat. Paul's leather pants hugged him tighter than his own skin. The pants didn't have a zipper to be unzipped.

I know. I was there.

I wasn't there to save my friend. I was back in my third floor hotel room, filing my review of the show for the glossy magazine that fired me this morning.

"You should have been there," they said. "You should have been the first one there."

Fuck. Me finding the bodies is the only thing that would have pleased those bastards. Making sure I took all the photos I could before telling anyone else would have earned me a bonus. My heirs—ha ha—could have spent the extra dough on my funeral. If I'd been there, I would have been just as dead as Steve and Vikk, with my brains plastered all over the ratty sofa in their dressing room.

Damn them. Those greedy tabloid fucks can rot in hell with every other rock star they've pushed over the edge.

Never make friends with the band. They tell you that your first day on the job.

Click.

"Jed, how long have we been friends?"

"Almost ten years. Since that first show at the Whiskey."

"Right. You know I can tell you everything and leave it

up to you to decide what gets printed and what doesn't."

"That's what we've always done, Syd."

"Well, I don't want you to tell anyone about this until tomorrow, please. Even better, tomorrow night. We'll be gone by then and you can write whatever you want. Just wait a little while on this one."

"Sure, Syd."

Click.

Just wait a little while on this one.
Just wait a little while…
Just wait…

#

They're dead. All of them. Nail Shitter is no more. No nasty break up played out in the tabloids. No need to talk about a reunion down the road and no potential for an embarrassing Super Bowl halftime show when they are sixty. Syd took out the entire band with a .357 Magnum. We should have heard the shots. Maybe someone did, but no one made it to his room in time to stop him from putting a rope around his neck and jumping off a table.

I should have been back there. I usually party all night when I'm with Nail Shitter. That night I decided to file my show review before getting hammered. I thought that if I got the review out as fast as possible, I wouldn't have a chance to write about the breakup. My editor might have given me hell if she found out I had a scoop and kept it to myself, but at that point, I was trying to honor the request of a friend. The breakup story would come later, and then I would get two by-lines and therefore two payments. Hey, I need to eat, too.

But I wasn't backstage and now I'm here listening to the voices of the dead. I am listening to Syd and not wondering if he'd planned on putting a bullet in my head, too. I should have been there. My friends are dead. I need a drink.

Voices Carry

Often I have a title before I have a story. "Voices Carry" went through a number of horrible titles before getting this final one. I like it and so it's staying.

If I ever did a series, Tom Royster would be the protagonist. The funny part is that he and I are more alike now than when I wrote this story. He drinks more than I do and is divorced, which I'm not. He also still lives in the middle of the Nevada desert, which I do not. He works at a community college, and I work at a university. When I wrote this story (longhand, in a fury, in a camping trailer), I was sending out stories and collecting rejections prior to starting college as a 23-year-old. If there's a lesson there, it is that it is never too late to start.

The story has its genesis in that remote Nevada town of about 150 residents, as does "Seeds and All," another of the older tales in this book. True stories often make the best—and scariest—fiction.

Perhaps we will see Tom Royster, community college journalism instructor and amateur ghost hunter, again.

The house doesn't stink anymore, but I can still see the bloodstains in the living room. The authorities wouldn't let me in that night. It has taken almost a month to convince the family to let me stay in the house. "It's not you," they said.

"It's just that… that… just… It's…" Then the crying started again.

I'm not unsympathetic. I believe in grieving. I also believe in a good story. And these things are best fresh.

At 6:30 p.m., December 23, John Allan went crazy. His wife Helen tried to stop him from killing the dogs. Her pleas for the three-week-old puppies came too late. She begged for the lives of the dogs.

After shooting his wife, John put a bullet in his stomach.

This is the official statement the White Pine County Sheriff's office gave me. This is the simple version. I want details.

The winter hasn't been as cold this year. Drought conditions throughout the Nevada High Desert have left the valley clear of snow. With no one to shovel the Allans' walk, the lack of snow is a blessing. Inside the house, with no one and no reason to use the woodstove, the cold has taken hold. Another mixed blessing; if this happened in the middle of summer, the house would smell like a butcher shop, even a month later.

The box next to the stove is full of chopped wood. The stove lengths came from the covered pile in the backyard. John Allan had prepared for a long winter.

I stood outside and watched the family remove all the food from the house. Contents of cupboards and the refrigerator were boxed up along with canned and bottled foods from the cellar. Helen Allan had prepared, too.

The furniture remains as Helen left it. I sit down in the recliner facing the television set. The frayed edges of a bullet hole scratch my spine. I grab the remote and press POWER The set comes on. I thought the electric company would have stopped service weeks ago. I flip through channels to see what is on.

The satellite company is quicker than the power people

are. I see more snow in five minutes than I have all winter. I can also see where blood has been wiped off the screen.

Unless you heard the shots, you didn't hear anything until someone called you. At 7:30 that night, my cousin Per called me. Per is a volunteer firefighter and EMT. He was called to the scene just as he was leaving for work.

Per told me no sirens were used because Sheriff King was in town and made it to the Allans' home first. By the time he arrived, everything except the fire was dead.

"How'd the Sheriff get the call if no one heard anything?" I asked.

"John called his brother in Washington right before shooting himself. The brother called here," Per told me. "Why didn't you hear the shots?"

Good question, I thought then. The Allans' house is right behind mine. Why didn't I hear the gunfire? The thin air often carries conversations throughout town. It was not unusual for me to hear John watching TV, especially during UNLV basketball games.

Sitting in John's chair, I can hear the trucks speeding by outside. I can hear Bobby Carson's ATV on the dirt road in front of my house.

I can hear someone's dog barking.

#

The Allans' new puppies were about twenty days old. Josie, the German shorthair mother, belonged to Helen. Fritz, the father, lives with Will Carson, father of four-wheeling Bobby, across town. He - Will, not Fritz - was present for the birth.

"There were nine of them," Will told me two weeks ago. "Cute as any newborn litter I ever saw. Even Johnny was smiling like a new daddy."

Nine puppies; the deputies couldn't tell one from

another when they arrived. And you complain about the piddle mess your puppy leaves.

I get up and walk into the kitchen. I'm glad to be out of John's chair. Sheriff King thinks John shot himself while sitting in the chair but died crawling to the front door. John didn't make it out.

The kitchen floor is spotless. I see the empty fridge, the dead stove, and the basket Josie slept in. The blankets were thrown out when the family cleaned the kitchen. They did a good job. I heard it took an entire day. They must have been tired and forgot to do as well in the living room.

I open the refrigerator and the light stays off. The fridge is warm and empty inside. Maybe it is unplugged, I think. Has to be; the TV came on.

I close the door and walk around the kitchen. Half of the puppies died in here, but you wouldn't know it by looking. Martha Stewart could do a show in here; it's that clean.

I move down the hall to the bedroom. The sheets are gone and the closets empty. The second bedroom is also empty. The Allans' twin girls, Tammie and Jenny, moved out over a decade before.

John Allan married Helen Clemm on April 20, 1969 at the Hotel Nevada in Ely, about 40 miles from where they would eventually die. He celebrated his twenty-first birthday six months later. Helen wouldn't be twenty-one for another year. In between, Tammie and Jenny were born. Helen had waited two years for John while he served his country. John stood, his arm in a sling from a bullet wound to the shoulder, and watched his bride walk down the aisle. He might have avoided the war altogether if he had married Helen instead of enlisting in the Army. They talked about it and decided together that John should join up and do what had to be done rather than risk leaving a family behind later.

John made it back. Helen stayed true to her promise to wait for him. Like with every serviceman, part of John died in

Southeast Asia. Unlike so many of our boys, John lived to see the next century.

It seems Charlie caught up with him two days before Christmas.

The sun is setting, and I'm still in the house. I'm planning to stay the night. I won't be using the sheetless bed. I'll be sleeping in the living room. On the couch where Helen Allan died.

I take a leak in the toilet and flush it. I rinse off my hands in the sink; no hot water. I shake off the excess water and wipe my hands on my pants. No towels, either.

I reach out to flip the hall light switch. The wall is freezing. I should have started a fire when I got here. Lucky for me, the power is still on.

I hit the switch and nothing happens. I flick it up and down, still nothing. I take the flashlight out of my jacket pocket and look at the light switch. It is in the ON position but the only light is from my flashlight.

I run to the kitchen and open the fridge. Dark, like before. I hold the flashlight under my arm and pull the fridge away from the wall. I get it out far enough to see that it is still plugged in.

I can't find the remote when I get to the living room. I almost trip over the bag I left by the chair. I hit the power button on the television set. Nothing.

Either I imagined the TV being on, or the power company has incredible timing. Both answers are displeasing.

Flashlight in hand, I make my way to the woodstove. I open the door and shine the light inside. It is clean of ashes. At least they left the wood next to the stove.

I take some paper from the stack by the wood. I crumple the old newspaper then toss it in the stove. I pile some smaller sticks on the paper then light a match. The newspaper catches quickly, and the twigs follow soon. Two stove lengths go in next, and I have a fire. Close the door.

Red light comes out of the glass front. Not enough to illuminate the room but enough to throw shadows.

The fire Helen started burned until the medical examiner from Las Vegas arrived early the next morning. People called the house to see what was happening. They wanted to know why they could still see smoke from the Allans' chimney. The same people will wonder why they see smoke tonight. The phone won't ring. I checked that myself. Even my cell phone is on silent mode.

Morbid as it sounds, I wanted to at least see inside the house that first night. I had taught more than one lecture course on urban legends, and I wanted to see how one might begin right from the start. I stood outside for three hours after Per called me, hoping to get inside. I left my camera at home but made sure to grab my notebook. I couldn't even peek through a window for a week.

The pictures from the sheriff's office are black and white. "To preserve the privacy of the deceased," they said. Doesn't bother me. I like black and white.

In the photos, the blood-smeared kitchen floor is black. Josie the dog is a dark lump in her basket. If you look close, you can see crushed and broken canine bones on the floor. John tracked a lot of blood into the living room. He took the last living dogs with him, too.

The blood on the television set is black on black. On the carpet, the blood is black on gray. The body of John Allan, covered in blood—less of his own than that of his wife and dogs—is identifiable because his left hand fell away from the door when Sheriff King entered the house. Most of the blood on John's arm rubbed off on the door.

Helen Allan's face stares out from the darkness. John cleaned her face before shooting himself. I can't see it in the pictures, but a rag lies next to her shoulder. He wiped off her hands as well. These are the whitest parts of the pictures. Except high up on the walls where no blood reached.

The living room walls have a yellowish tint, some from blood splatter, most from the years John smoked in the house. The furniture and carpet have been shampooed. Dark spots still show, and the bullet holes haven't been repaired.

Why didn't they take the living room furniture when they cleaned? And why move it back to the same places when they were done?

Why take anything? Why even bother to clean in the first place?

Tammie and Jenny won't talk to me anymore, so I can't ask them.

Back in high school, I dated both of them. The overlap lasted a week. I went out with Tammie three weeks before and with Jenny five weeks after. It wasn't until my break up with Jenny that they both decided to hate me. You can't leave one twin for another without the first twin hating you. You can't date the second twin for long without her hating you, too.

They are both married now. I dealt with their husbands to get my access. Apparently, Tammie and Jenny still hate me. I did nothing to ease that fury by trying to get into their dead parents' house. I'm pretty sure their respective husbands hate me now. I'm in the house, though, so what does it matter?

I put three candles on the windowsill behind the couch and light them. With the candles and the light from the stove, I can see well enough not to bump into the recliner. I walk back to the stove and throw in another log. If I were home, I would be doing the same thing: keeping up the fire, lounging on the couch, downing a couple of beers, and watching the tube.

Up at five in the morning and head to Great Basin Community College where I teach English 101 and the occasional special topic.

No beer tonight and no school tomorrow.

I step on the remote control while walking back to the

couch. The TV clicks on, and the room fills with jumpy light. Black blobs cross the screen, splitting and mixing with the snow. I bend down and grab the control. I press the power button, and the TV turns off. I hit it again, and the TV turns on. The black splotches have spread but somehow seem brighter than before. I step to the set and push the manual power button. Off goes the set. I push the button again.

Nothing.

I push the remote power button, and the TV comes back on but is now filled with the luminescent darkness. As I stare into the screen, I begin to hear a soft, animalistic whimpering. A sound like young fur rubbing on rougher, older fur. When the screaming starts, I turn the set off again and throw the remote on the recliner.

Maybe I should have brought a six-pack.

I reach into my bag and pull out a candy bar. I open it and toss the wrapper on top of the stack of newspapers. I wonder how many of my stories the Allans burned in their stove.

The whole town for that matter.

#

"A lot, Tommy."

Did I say that out loud? My lips moved but the voice wasn't mine.

"Don't go getting bonkers, Tom," I say. Out loud and on purpose. "It isn't even 6:30 yet. You can't be spooked before kill time."

I shake my head and slap myself a couple times. I go to the couch and lie down. My left thumb pokes into a bullet hole. I can still hear that dog barking outside, and the noises from the TV hang in the air.

The headlight on Bobby Carson's four-wheeler broke in October, so he doesn't drive at night. Most of the big rigs have come and gone.

Other than that dog, the entire town is silent. If the townspeople weren't all scared, I bet they would be outside waiting for me to come running out the front door, screaming.

Not tonight, sorry. Go on home, folks. Nothing to see here. Move it along.

And someone please shut that dog up.

#

"Helen, would you please shut that dog up!"

"Calm down. She's still healing, give her a break."

"God damn it! Now she's got those mutts screaming too. They haven't clammed up since they were born. I can't stand it. Crying all night and day, scratching around and making all that noise. I hear it all the time and I can't take it anymore. It has to stop."

I'm asleep on the couch. I recognize John Allan's voice. I see myself.

I walk to the closet and get my .45 and the three full clips. I'm John Allan and I'm always prepared.

"John, what are you doing? Put that gun away."

I stare at my wife, Helen. I walk past her into the kitchen. She screams as I put four bullets into Josie, her German Shorthair.

"John, what are you doing? Stop! Don't kill the dogs, John. Stop it, please."

I shove Helen away from me. She stumbles into the living room and falls onto the couch. She is still screaming.

I grab two dogs and hoist them into the air then throw them down to the floor. The barking doesn't stop. More dogs, too many. I grab another and mash its puppy face in the bones of its brothers.

"Shut up, Helen. Shut the hell up," I scream as I cover

the floor with dog guts. I shoot three of the monsters and pull their insides out through the bullet holes. I throw entrails at Helen, standing in the living room. She won't stop screaming.

"Please, Johnny, don't hurt the puppies. Don't hurt me. Please, John, don't."

I grasp her by the hair and push her down on the couch. She doesn't stop yelling until I empty the rest of the clip into her chest.

I, me, Tom Royster, community college instructor and first-time ghost hunter, wake up screaming. My candles are out, and the fire is weak. The living room is lit by the television.

John Allan sits in his recliner, gun in one hand and telephone in the other. His lips are moving but I can't hear anything. No words, no barking, no gunfire.

John sets the phone on its cradle and picks up the remote control. I can't see the picture on the screen. The TV is covered with blood.

John pushes the power button on the remote, and the room becomes dark. He looks toward me and sees his wife. I see her, face and hands free of blood, and get up. I lean against the door, trying to get out. The door won't budge.

John Allan aims the gun at his stomach and fires. He stands up, adding his own blood to the mess. He heads for the door.

"It's so quiet, finally," I hear him say. "I have to tell everyone about the quiet." His empty hand hits my shoulder. He slips on dog bowels and falls. The gun goes off. The bullet hits John in the ear.

The door opens and I fall on my ass. No one is out here to see me fall. I look back into the house. I can't see anything. The candles burned out and the fire died. The TV is off.

Outside it is dark. It is quiet. Almost.

Somewhere I can hear a dog barking and a soft whimpering, floating on the air and right into my brain.

Shut that damn dog up," I yell as I run back to my house. "SHUT UP!"

#

My house is empty when I get there. The house has been empty every night since my wife left me four years ago. She never liked Great Basin City, the desert scrub town I still live in with fewer than three hundred other people. *What kind of place calls itself a city when there's only one store and no stoplights?* she would always say.

The kind of place that doesn't notice a man sneaking back into a haunted house, I'd tell her now. After she stopped laughing at me, that is.

My first real ghost and I ran. Over thirty years of cheap horror novels and cheaper horror movies and I ran.

It is two in the morning. So far, I'm the only person who knows I left the Allan house screaming. Nobody heard the shots that night, why would they hear me? I could go back now and no one would be the wiser. As I finish my fifth beer, I remind myself I need to get my bag. I left it sitting next to John Allan's recliner.

I convince myself that I can walk out the front door – bag in hand, smile on face—at exactly 7:00 a.m. Just in time for the couple morning joggers to see me.

Give me a night with two ghosts and call me crazy; catch me jogging at seven on Saturday and shoot me.

I take the last bottle of the six-pack and my flashlight with me. Thank You, God, for not letting me drop the flashlight. Thank you, Mom, for making me sit through all those horror movies no matter how scared I got.

Scare me once, shame on you.

I make it back to the former (and still) home of John

and Helen Allan not quite as fast as I ran away from it mere hours before. The house is dark, as any house of deceased residents should be. I have my flashlight on and a book of matches in my pocket. I left the empty beer bottle by the fence. Nothing should have disturbed the candles I left on the windowsill. I hope.

I open the door and go straight to the candles. It takes five matches, but eventually the three candles give me enough light to feel comfortable. I look at the woodstove but do not start another fire. My candy bar wrapper sits right where I left it.

In the candlelight, I can't see the bloodstains. I can't see the bullet holes in the couch or the recliner, either. The TV stays dark, too.

I go to the kitchen and bring back a chair from the table out to the living room. I can stay in the house, I think, but no way am I sitting on that bullet-ridden couch or the recliner, its one bullet hole like the opening of a shark's mouth.

I place the chair against the front door then grab my bag. I sit down with the bag on my lap. I stare at my candles —away from the TV—until I fall asleep. No dreams of irate husbands killing their wives or their wives' dogs. I haven't even heard that stupid dog barking since my third beer back home. Goodnight, doggie, be glad you'll see tomorrow.

I dream instead, sleeping on that kitchen chair, of my wife, Natalie. I dream of her being dead. Not in any hate-filled way, rather in a tragic way. My dream is of her dying before she can leave me. Her death giving me a reason to be a ghost hunter instead of a burden on the higher education system. The former teacher coping with the passing of his beloved spouse by tracking down other "displaced spirits" hoping someday to meet his wife again.

I know; you've read it in too many pulp novels and seen it countless times on screen, both black and white and color. My ex-wife is not dead. She spends way too much money to be resting in peace.

I wake up with the sun hitting my face and pools of wax on the windowsill. My neck is stiff, and my bag has fallen off my lap. A pile of candy bars spills over one foot. I reach down to get a candy bar and look at my watch simultaneously – 9:30, in black LED. I made it. I stand up, munching chocolaty peanuts. I move my head around and pop my neck. In the sunlight streaming through the windows, I can't see the bloodstains or the bullet holes.

Maybe I imagined them. Maybe I imagined everything. Maybe I should stay another night, just to be sure. Then I can find other ghosts.

Perhaps someone will die tonight. Plenty of elderly folks in town.

After all, these things are best fresh.

Hath No Fury

Of my previously unpublished short work, "Hath No Fury" is my favorite. Ciera Hale is the most badass woman I have written and the one who feels the most realized. She could walk into my office right now and it wouldn't surprise me, but I would wonder what she wanted.

And as much as I love "Hath No Fury," I also know that it is very much a product of its time and influence, namely Quentin Tarantino circa 2005. Read it; watch some Tarantino and you'll see. And if you think I ripped him off too much, all I can say is watch more Tarantino. He'd understand.

There is a good chance that Trent Hale, Ciera's murdered husband, was employed by the same company the nameless letter-writer from "Hemingway at Work" worked for.

Transfer your suffering to those who deserve it. Your pain, caused by another, should not be yours alone to bear. Take the fire of torment that burns in your soul and light the flames of vengeance. Bring torture and despair to those responsible for your own despair. Take life for life. And more.

Start with those you know, the two police officers who arrived first at the scene, the ones you know were there too soon. They will tell you where to go next.

Part One: Buckley

Sparks and howls followed Ciera Hale as she left the Rogue Saloon. Bottles of booze continued to explode while being consumed by the spreading fire. Soon, the entire building would be one big barbecue pit: gristle seared to the top, bones mixed with the ashes of the wood frame building. It was comforting to know that at least one pig, probably two, fried along with their junkie informants and pimp consorts. The smell of burning cop is indistinguishable from the smell of burning prostitute. They all smell bad.

They scream differently, Hale had learned. The hookers, not all of them cry. Most seemed to expect something like this to happen. One pimp hit a girl when she couldn't find a way out of the carnage. Hale shot him before she shot the girl. The cop, the one she was certain of, he cried. Squealed, Hale thought, as she pressed her gun into his eye. He never tried to reach for his piece. Instead, he grabbed his crotch, trying to not let the stream of urine escape into his pants. All the rest, the bouncers, the junkies, the mumbling winos, mixed into one chorus of shared pain.

Hale didn't shoot all of them, not at first. She shot the bouncers, so they couldn't bother her beyond the door. She shot the bartender when he reached under the bar for a shotgun. She shot a thug by the jukebox when he made a move to skin a pistol from beneath his leather jacket. Then it was fists and feet.

The bikers, friends of the dead guy by the jukebox, rushed her. Four hirsute, odoriferous men pounced on her, a variety of blunt objects ready to attack. Hale absorbed her share of blows but dished out more. If a pipe connected with her abdomen, she knocked out teeth in return. A chair hit her in the back of the head; she used the momentum to fall into the neck of another brute, clamping her teeth on the dirty, loose skin she found there. She did not let go; the chunk of flesh stayed in her mouth when another biker pulled her off his comrade. A stream of blood spanned the space between Hale's mouth and the fallen goon. She turned and spat the freed skin into the face of the man who last touched her. He clawed at his cheeks to get away from the piece of his dead friend. Hale planted a kick to his scrotum and he fell to the ground, out of the fight.

One thug picked up a table to slam down on her. A dropped Zippo touched a shot of vodka and the fire started. The crowd, never very big, moved into a corner of the bar, near the restrooms. Hale expected frightened cattle, ready to stampede. Instead she saw human sheep herding themselves.

With the herd in the corner, Hale shifted her attention to Buckley. He never moved from his seat at the bar. He had plenty of time to take her out with a shot in the back, but he didn't take the chance. Tears began to form in his eyes before Hale put a hand on his shoulder and spun him around to face her.

Buckley, never man enough to face a woman like Ciera Hale, blurted out, "I'm sorry. Please don't kill me."

Hale raised her gun, the barrel still hot from shooting the thug at the jukebox, and brought it to within an inch of Buckley's left eye. "Why," she asked. "Why did you take my family?"

"I didn't, it was all Jensen," Buckley said. Hale moved the gun another quarter inch closer to his eyeball. She grabbed him by the collar with her other hand and sat on his thighs when he tried to squirm away.

"Jensen is dead. He told me you did it."

"That fucking liar! I'm going to kick his ass!" Hale closed the space between the gun and Buckley's eye. His high-pitched wail attracted the attention of the herd. Hale's body obscured Buckley's from their vision. If it weren't for the fire and the scream, it might have looked like Hale was just another pro plying her trade.

"I told you Jensen is dead. Do I need to clean out your ears?" Hale let go of Buckley's collar and pulled back her coat, exposing a twelve-inch-long butcher knife. "I have the right tool. Jensen heard perfectly just before I used it to cut his throat."

Buckley glanced at the knife with his free eye. Hale noticed something like recognition ticking in his eyes.

"What have you done to my wife?" Buckley cried. He began pistoning his hips, trying to throw Hale off his body.

"Nothing you and Jensen didn't do to Trent. Nothing you didn't do to my little Lisa."

Buckley's face, already pale, went paper white. "I didn't want to do it. We had to. Menks gave the order and Jensen couldn't get it up." Menks. Menks would be next and then it would be over.

"She was only ten," Hale said, pushing the gun barrel farther into Buckley's eye socket. "You raped her and murdered her all while her daddy watched. So I went to see your wife. She really liked this knife."

"Fuck you, you cunt," Buckley threw his hips up at Hale, a desperate parody of the acts each had committed. Hale slipped off his legs but kept the gun in place. She stood up, pulling Buckley's sweat-drenched body next to hers. She felt his hands on his crotch then, at first thinking he was going to show her what got him in trouble. Instead, the aroma of fresh urine wafted into her nose, mixing with the smells of gunpowder, alcohol, fire, and fear.

"No, Buckley. Fuck you." She tilted her head and kissed him on the lips. She pulled the trigger as she disengaged from the kiss, sending Buckley's head rocking on his neck. Hair, skull, blood, and brain matter splashed on the bottles and mirror behind the bar. His body went down, taking the stool he sat on with it.

The reflection of fire in the parts of the mirror and bottles not covered in pieces of Buckley caught Hale by surprise. She had almost forgotten the fire and the people cowering behind it. She saw the pimp hit his girl because she would not jump through the fire. Hale shot him first, then the girl.

Hale put the last five rounds of the clip into random bodies behind the flames. They would all die in the fire, she thought, so speeding up the process would be merciful wouldn't it?

She reloaded then holstered the gun. She began turning the still-standing tables into the fire, more wood for the flames. Then she went behind the bar. She had to step over the bartender's body to get to most of the good, flammable alcohol. It only took four bottles thrown into the flames to urge the flames to touch the ceiling. The sheep—all those pimps, pros, junkies, and drunks—could only be heard now.

Hale moved out from behind the bar, and walked toward the door. She grabbed the bartender's shotgun on her way. Before exiting, Hale turned around and fired the shotgun into the cacophony. Some voices became louder; some stopped.

She exited the bar, and still heard screams of pain trying to reach someone who could end it and the tongues of fire reaching for more material to engulf. Some of the people inside the bar might have been innocent. Most of them didn't know Buckley was a cop. Most of them didn't even know who Buckley was. Hale had taught them a lesson in suffering at an extreme level. They huddled inside the burning bar: the shot, the burnt, the scared, all paying the price for too much indulgence in the things that cause upset to the mind.

Part Two: Jensen

Hale spent a year trying to forget the deaths of her husband and child and another three years preparing to claim her revenge before spending the last four weeks watching

Jensen and Buckley. Tracking every move, recording each routine. Knowing when they were together and when they were not. Jensen spent his off-duty time home, while Buckley cavorted with lowlifes at the Rogue. She decided to take out Jensen first.

Two days before the massacre at the Rogue Saloon, Ciera broke into Buckley's house, taking with her the long butcher knife. The next day, she broke into Jensen's three-room bungalow. She waited for him in the bedroom, curtains drawn, holding the knife in one hand and her gun in the other. It was 11:30 a.m. when she closed the door of Jensen's room; she knew he would not end his shift until 5 p.m. Unlike the married Buckley, Jensen always came straight home after work. He had every night for the last four weeks, Hale reminded herself. Waiting five hours would be nothing compared to the four years previous. Nothing she had planned for him would compare to the hell of knowing he had participated in the murder of her husband, Trent, and the rape and murder of her ten-year-old girl, Lisa. But she would do her worst.

Hale spent much of that time doing the same thing she'd done for most of the last four years: asking herself why, questioning the reasons behind the death of her family, wishing she did not have to be waiting for the man who killed her husband.

She wandered around Jensen's room. His high school, college, and police academy diplomas hung on the wall over a chest of drawers. There were no pictures in this room, not even any cheap framed art prints. There was a large closet, almost as big as the room. A good place to hide, maybe. The double-sized bed with nightstands on each side dominated the rest of the room. The bed was tightly made, as if a machine pulled the covers back up each morning. There was no litter on the floor and the small wastebasket beneath one nightstand was empty. Such a clean freak, Hale thought, for someone who made such a mess of her life.

Hale resisted the urge to pull the blankets and sheets off the bed, to turn over the mattress, to empty the drawers after looking inside each of them. As much as she wanted to destroy Jensen's existence, she knew messing with this room would not help her now. Maybe later, after he was dead.

After sifting through Jensen's drawers, she allowed herself to lie back on the bed and gaze at the ceiling with its near-pure whiteness. A blank slate, like her life could have become. Hale lost everything at the hands of Jensen and Buckley. She hated the idea that her entire life could be wiped out by two second-rate detectives, one who cared nothing for the seemingly perfect life he had and the other who seemed to have no life at all.

Years spent away from everything she knew couldn't keep her from needing her family. Yet even when she decided what she had to do, she knew she wasn't ready. During the second year, traveling the word, letting her rage build to the point that she could face the men who introduced chaos into her life and turned her into a person so different from the woman she knew, she almost gave up. Hale almost talked herself into letting go. It would have been so easy to take one of the guns she trained herself to use and press in against her own temple or put it into her mouth.

Or she could get even. With everyone. It wasn't just Buckley and Jensen; she knew others must be involved. Neither of these cops were smart enough (or stupid enough) to perpetrate such heinous acts. Someone was pulling their strings, making them dance like degenerate marionettes. Until she knew who was behind it all, everyone would suffer. If she had to burn down the entire city, Hale would have her revenge.

The sound of a door opening caused Hale to sit back up in her first position, gun in her right hand, knife in her left. No time to hide in that big closet, she thought. No hiding anywhere. She coiled herself on the bed, ready to spring the moment Jensen opened the door to his bedroom. Instead, she could hear him wandering around his small kitchen and smaller living room.

Get in here. Get in here. Get in here. The mantra spun through Hale's mind, helping her focus on the door. Jensen's footfalls neared the door then stopped. Did he sense something amiss? Did he imagine death breathing down his neck while in reality it awaited him on the other side of the door?

GET IN HERE. Hale had to hold herself back from jumping at the door before it started opening. Time was up, no more waiting.

Jensen's foot pushed the door ajar, and then his head was visible. He entered the room reading his mail when he should have been more observant. No one, Hale thought, ever thinks something bad will happen in their own home, not even cops. He looked up just in time to see Hale leaping off his bed, swinging the junior machete at him.

Hale caught him in the forearm with the knife then pushed her gun under his chin. She could feel Jensen trying to talk, maybe scream, but she pushed harder so he couldn't open his mouth. Blood from the gash in his arm sprayed on his floor and his cabinet, some splattering the glass of his framed diplomas.

Without directly touching Jensen, Hale moved him to the bed, manipulating his movements with her gun and the knife still stuck in his arm. Jensen continued to try to scream, but each time he tried to open his mouth, Hale pressed the gun deeper into the soft flesh there. When she had him sitting on the bed with his back to the wall, Hale removed the knife from Jensen's arm then plunged it through his shirt, stabbing through his trapezius muscle, near the neck. That bulging muscle she hated on the pro wrestlers, she thought. The one that really made them look unnatural. The muscles

Trent had spent his mornings trying to bulk up.

Jensen's trapezius was not as well-developed as a pro wrestler's, or even as developed as Trent's had been, but there was enough muscle there to help pin him to the wall. Hale hit the handle of the knife with the palm of her hand, pushing it in more. Jensen finally screamed loud enough to cause Hale to lighten the pressure of the gun under his chin.

"You fucking bitch. I'm going to kill you." The pain added a tremor to Jensen's voice that Hale could not recall hearing in any of his previously overheard conversations.

"You've killed enough people for one lifetime, don't you think?" Hale kept her left hand wrapped around the handle of the knife and holstered her gun with her right hand. She traced the outline of the gun barrel, sights and all, that formed the better part of the bruise blackening on Jensen's skin. "I don't think you will be killing anyone else ever again."

"Who the hell do you think you are?"

Hale stopped tracing the bruise and pushed instead. Jensen winced, bouncing his head against the wall. That shook the knife piercing him to the wall and he screamed again.

"I wouldn't move around too much if I were in your position, Jensen. Mrs. Buckley keeps her cutlery extra sharp, and if you squirm, that knife is likely to cut right through the muscle. Might even shift and slice right into your neck. We wouldn't want that to happen, would we? Well, not yet, anyway." A small remnant of mercy tugged at her, telling her to end it soon. Then she pictured Trent and Lisa, her smiling, happy family, silently wading in the pools of their own blood.

"What do you want?"

"I want to know why you murdered my husband. I want to know why you raped and murdered my baby girl."

"I don't even know you. Who are you?"

There was no letting go. Not now, not ever.

Hale twisted the knife before she spoke again. "You know me. I watched you smirking at the inquest. I saw you high-five that bastard Buckley as you left the courtroom without a hint of suspicion aimed at you. Just two cops who showed up at the wrong time, just a little too late to save my family.

"Then I saw you get into your car. It was the same car I saw parked near the corner when I left for work that morning."

Jensen sat, blood running down his body, and said the only thing that came to mind. "You weren't supposed to go to work that day. Buckley did all the work on your daughter, but I think I would have got a hard-on for you." He took the brief second of Hale's silence to throw a punch at her face. She dodged the misguided punch, throwing her body off the bed.

With her body came her left hand, still holding the knife. More blood exploded from Jensen as the knife vacated its sheath of flesh. He held a hand to the wound, attempting to stop the bleeding. Even injured Jensen's cop reflexes still worked. He moved fast, opening the drawer of a nightstand and pulling out a small pistol.

"Bitch," Jensen said. "You should have been dead already but I'll finish you right here. I'll drag your body to Menks and no one will ever know what happened to you." He aimed the gun at Hale's face and pulled the trigger.

A loud click hit Hale's ears but no bullet touched her.

"You stupid pig," Hale said, standing up and facing Jensen dead on. "How long do you think I've been waiting for you? You didn't think I just sat here without going through your drawers, did you? I know about you and Buckley. I even know about Menks."

This was a lie. The information that Daniel Menks, Trent's boss, had something to do with this was new to Hale.

"Go to Hell," Jensen yelled then threw his useless gun

at Hale. Like with his earlier punch, Hale easily dodged the thrown object. Jensen turned his back on her, but there was nowhere left for him to go. She walked up next to him and put her right arm around his body. She lifted his head and started kissing the side of his neck that wasn't bleeding.

"I've been in Hell for four years," she said, bringing the knife up to his throat. "Let me show you the way."

#

Hale didn't stay to mess up Jensen's house any more than it already was. The blood pouring from his slit throat would be hard enough to clean up on its own. Besides, she still had more bacon to fry.

Part Three: Trent and Lisa

Detectives Buckley and Jensen weren't in the car when Ciera Hale walked by on her way to work. If they had been, the last four years of Hale's life would have been different. She often wondered exactly how different. She might be dead, lying in a coffin next to her husband and her child. Perhaps Trent and Lisa would be living still, enjoying the ups and downs of suburban life, going to school plays, watching wrestling matches, and paying off credit cards.

That isn't how things turned out, Hale reminded herself as she stood over the graves of her family. It was cheaper to etch her name into the headstone at the same time as the names and dates for Trent and Lisa. No one she knew expected her to recover from the shock. She didn't know whether anyone had been looking for her after she left the hospital. It didn't matter. She wasn't the same person, not really.

She had a life many would want: a loving husband who worked for a pharmaceutical company, a daughter who wanted to be an actress when she grew up, and a steady, low-pressure job as a grocery store cashier. She had always thought she would have plenty of time with her family. She was wrong about so many things.

She never thought of asking Trent what he did at MenkLabs. The three of them would be sitting in front of the TV, usually watching the Friday night wrestling matches, and Trent would point out commercials for the drugs he help create.

"My little part to make the world better for you," he'd tell Lisa. Something from that world reached out and killed both of them. A part of herself, Ciera Hale as she once thought of herself, died as well.

After killing Jensen, Buckley, and the people in the Rogue Saloon, and paying a special visit to Buckley's wife, any innocence Hale ever had was long dead. Hale wasn't sure if she could come back from that, if she could ever again be the person she once was: a wife, a mother, a lover. Not this sadistic, gun-toting, hell bitch.

Hale wondered exactly what part Menks played in the chaos of her life. What could Trent have known or done that would bring this kind of fury into her life? Had she always been this person? Was that why she loved the gratuitous violence she saw on TV?

Both Jensen and Buckley implied that Menks had given the order. Menks would be the last. Then she could rest.

But would it make her whole again? Killing these people had not mended Trent's flayed body. Ending lives would not bring back Lisa to her mother, still whole, not raped, beaten, and shot. None of this could take Hale back to the day she took the early Sunday morning phone call, asking her to cover for a coworker at the grocery store. Nothing could take her back to the time when kick-boxing classes were just exercise, not something she would have to use on another person. Nothing she could ever do would bring back her family.

She knelt on the soft cemetery grass, crying, laying her weapons next to her. Her head, slightly singed from the saloon fire, touched the cold marble. Tears pooled in the numerals of her daughter's birthday as Hale thought of all the parties Lisa would never have. She traced the letters of her husband's name, wishing to run her fingers along the lines of his body again.

Hale remembered seeing them for the last time, playing together, like nothing could touch them. She remembered seeing all the red that came out of them, like spilled paint, soaking into the carpet. Seeing Trent in the middle of the living room flayed out like a bearskin rug. She remembered finding Lisa in the bathtub, all the blood covering her like the clothes she should have had on.

Two sets of footprints went from the bathroom to the living room with a set of tracks between them that looked like skis. During the inquest, the coroner said these were made by Trent's dragging feet after he was forced to watch the rape of his daughter then taken by the unknown assailants to the living room where his throat was cut with a large, never recovered, butcher knife.

Hale knew the assailants now and both were headed for plots of their own. Buckley's body had been identified when his badge was found among the rubble of the Rogue Saloon. When investigators went to inform Jensen, they found his body on the bed, spread out like a blanket of spent flesh. Buckley's wife was listed as missing and wanted for questioning.

It was only a few days, but Hale assumed the cops were putting things together, much faster than they did for her own family. Jensen and Buckley, both dead. Buckley's wife, only missing as far as the police knew. The deaths of police officers—even bad ones, she thought— caused things to move at a higher pace than regular, everyday homicide. Hale wondered if the police might already be on her trail, closing in on her as she communed with her family.

She relaxed her body and fell asleep on the graves of her family.

#

If she had been awake, she would have known someone was on her trail and moving in. She didn't feel a thing when the needle pierced her jeans and then the skin of her thigh. Peace had become such a foreign thing that Hale accepted it as a dream, wanting it to last as long as possible before she awoke again to the nightmare her life had become.

Part Four: Menks

She woke up in the dark. The coolness of the headstone was replaced with the dry warmth of a hood. Her hands were bound but her feet were free. She tried to stand up but a rush of dizziness caused her to sit back down. Panic wanted to take over, but she held it back, breathing as well as she could through the hood.

Focus, focus. Listen. Smell. Two men, heavy steppers, circling her. One smoking a cigarette, the other chewing gum. Big men, both. With the dizziness, Hale did not dare make a move. She would have to concentrate on not panicking and wait to see what happened. She closed her eyes and welcomed back the darkness.

A short time later, she felt one of those heavy feet kick her in the thigh. "Wake up, bitch. Someone wants to talk to you." She did not recognize the voice, but she would not forget it.

"I'm awake. Don't kick me again unless you want to lose that foot."

"Such a petty threat, Mrs. Hale." Menks; the first voice

she knew. "You don't want me to have Johnny kill you with that hood still on, do you?"

"Menks, I don't make petty threats. I took out Buckley and Jensen, didn't I? I'm going to kill you and these two bozos, also."

"Ciera, Ciera, calm down, please." Menks pulled the hood off Hale's head. "You are much too beautiful to be so angry." He ran his fingers along her cheek, looking into her eyes.

"Don't you fucking touch me. There's blood on your hands whether you did the killing or not. You aren't going to leave this room."

"No? What are you going to do to if I want to leave?" Menks smirked, leaning into Hale's face. "What are you going to do?"

Hale lunged out, clamping her teeth into Menks's cheek. He pulled back, trying to get away but Hale held on. She saw both men pull guns. She moved into the corner, putting Menks between herself and the gunmen.

She reached into his jacket, where she knew he always carried a gun. She found his .38 with her bound hands. She pushed Menks around with her shoulder, never letting go of his cheek. The goons were still looking for a shot that wouldn't hit Menks. Hale hid the gun between their bodies and fired blindly. She heard the groans and the falling bodies. One gun went off when it hit floor, followed by the sound of a bullet penetrating a meaty thigh.

Hale pushed Menks away from her. She looked at her hands, seeing they were bound only with tape. She bit through the tape much easier than she had bitten through Menks's cheek. Once her hands were free, she went back to Menks.

He sat on the floor, holding his bleeding face, eyes wide. She stood over him, the one in power, just like she had been with everyone she'd killed up to now. She could sense how certain people become addicted to this feeling. Knowing you hold the lives of men and women in your hands, controlling the destiny of even one person. If she ever wanted to be herself again, she knew she would have to let go of her rage.

She located the door and moved near it, stepping over the two newly dead bodies. Menks reached out and grabbed her by the ankle.

"Don't you want to know why," he asked, holding her with one hand and his mangled face with the other. "Don't you want to know?"

"I told you not to touch me," Hale said. Without looking at Menks, lying prostrate on the floor of his own abattoir, she shot him in the head. His grip on her ankle loosened then let go. She dropped the gun on his back. She faced the door again, not knowing exactly where it led. She opened it and walked out.

Part Five: Ciera

It's hard, some days, not knowing why she is still alive and her family isn't. There isn't a day that she doesn't think about it. Menks wanted to tell her, but she shot him. Whatever the reason, it wouldn't bring them back. No reason would do her family justice. Nothing, she realized, could bring them back.

She would hear people whisper as she walked by them on the streets. *She looks so haunted. What could have happened to make her look like that?* If she looked back at the whisperers, they would scuttle off like scared dogs. No one looked her in the eyes anymore. She wouldn't look anyone else in the eyes, either. If she didn't see Trent or Lisa, she would see one of the people she killed. It was best just to not see anyone.

Seeds and All

"Seeds and All" is the second story inspired by my time living in small-town Nevada. Walking through cemeteries can give one all sorts of ideas. This piece gelled after just such a walk.

When I was a student at the Community College of Southern Nevada, I took this story to a national conference and read it there. I learned two things from that reading: this is a tear-jerker and horror can come from anywhere. The first is obvious. There were not many dry eyes in the room and at the following year's conference I met multiple people who remembered me for this story. That felt pretty darn good.

The second thing should have been obvious to me then and is something I took to heart. After reading, I talked briefly about how the story came to life and mentioned that it was a very different story for me because I usually wrote horror. A gentleman then asked, "Are you sure this isn't horror?"

Keep that in mind as you read. And if you shed a tear or two, that's fine.

If they'd been older, maybe things'd been different. If they'd been eighteen or twenty, gone off to live their lives, it wouldn't have been so bad. I like to think of them like that:

John married to a local girl and working the farm, Wendy in school, studying hard and dating a future doctor. Sometimes I like to think of Wendy being the doctor and John traveling the world doing something, anything. Those "what ifs" are great fun while I'm thinking them. Afterwards, I'm always stuck with the plain old truth.

As it goes, the truth is this: they were cousins, born a month and a half apart; grown-up as each other's shadow; separated in death by mere hours. The core of the apple holds the seeds, my grandma used to say, but how many people you know eat the core?

This all began in 1926. My mama told us she was with child, had been for about three months. We were all there: me, Pa, Grandma, Uncle Lane, and Aunt Arlene. So after Mama gave us her news, Aunt Arlene stood and echoed Mama. The only difference being that Aunt Arlene was only six weeks sure instead of three months. I was about to lose the honor not just of being an only child but an only grandchild as well. Which was fine by me; two more bodies helping with the chores that had recently become my responsibility was peachy keen in my mind. As long as they were both boys.

Six months later, half my wish came true. Mama gave birth to John, my little brother. Grandma and Aunt Arlene stayed with her the whole time. Uncle Lane swore he could hear Mama screaming from the alfalfa field. Pa didn't say nothing. Childbirth was still a scary thing in those days with no assurance that the mother would survive. Luckily, Mama made it through and was recovered enough to repay Aunt Arlene by being with her during her first delivery.

I miss Aunt Arlene, too. Not as much as I miss John and Wendy and not as much as Uncle Lane missed her. I was five years old at the time and had seen horses and cattle put down as well as my first dog. Aunt Arlene, though. I remember she looked more beautiful in her coffin than I had ever seen her before. Even at Christmas. Uncle Lane was always saying that Wendy looked just like her mother. Uncle Lane also cried more than any other man I've ever known.

John and Wendy might as well have been twins. They each began life suckling at Mama's breast. Two peas in a pod was how the townsfolk always talked about them. Kids at school took to calling me the head pea, which quickly turned into pea-head. I didn't mind; taking a ribbing is part of being a kid. John and Wendy had it worse.

When you're six and someone mentions you're kissing cousins, it's cute and all the old people laugh. If John and Wendy had made it into the higher grades in school, being called "kissing cousins" would have been the end of any social life. Things like that just don't seem so important now. Another thing Grandma always said was, "When you've got family this close, who needs friends?" John and Wendy didn't need anyone but each other.

A few weeks before John's eighth birthday, I found the two of them out in the orchard. They were sprawled on the ground, on opposite sides of a tree. Apples, some eaten to the core, some only half-gone, covered the patch of earth between them.

"I think I ate too many," Wendy said, her mouth containing the last bites of an autumn fruit.

"I think I ate more than you," John said. At least, that is what I think he said. He was still taking mouthfuls from the apple in his hand. I have never seen an apple as green as those two faces. Wendy had eaten most of the apples I was witness to the remains of. John, who indeed did eat more, did not stop at the core.

We could hear John bellowing "Seeds and all, seeds and all" from the outhouse for a week.

#

We always celebrated John's and Wendy's birthdays together, even being six weeks apart. They were good parties, considering the times. The whole family needed that one happy day a year. When Wendy's real birthday came around, no one said anything. Uncle Lane would stay in his room all day. (One year, I believe it was Wendy's third birthday, no one saw Uncle Lane for a whole week. Everyone in the house could hear him, though. Crying all night and sobbing all day.) The week before and the week following were hard days in our house. Uncle Lane was extra sweet to Wendy after her birthday, but sometimes he got mean to her before. He never hit her, not that anyone knew. I guess it's hard for a man to look upon the child that caused his wife's death, especially when the child looked so much like her mother.

Somehow, John and Wendy remained sheltered from the Depression. I kept busy helping Pa and Uncle Lane in the fields and orchards and feeding and milking the one cow we didn't sell. Those two, though, always seemed to be playing around. Keeping each other safe from the world, that's how Grandma put it.

One night I overheard Uncle Lane saying he was glad Aunt Arlene didn't live to see these times. That it was best for her to have passed because she'd just be another mouth to try and feed.

That was the only night I ever saw Grandma get angry.

"Lane Thomas Hendrix, how in God's name you say such a thing? I suppose you'd just as soon have sweet Wendy never born. Or your own mother in the grave. Just another mouth to feed! If your father, who made it his business to feed every hungry soul he could, heard you say such a thing. You know exactly what he'd do. You're still my child, answer me."

"Damn, Ma…" Lane started, then SMACK! The impact of Grandma's hand on Uncle Lane's face made me swear to heaven never to make her mad at me.

"You watch your filthy mouth talking like that. This is still my house and I won't have it. I won't have anyone talking about being glad someone ain't around, either. We all need to be thanking Lord Jesus for what we do have and be willing to share with those that don't have. Am I understood?"

"Yes, Ma," said Uncle Lane. I'm guessing that his head hung low saying it.

"Am I understood?" she said again.

"Yes, Ma," I heard Pa say. Those were the only words he said since Grandma spoke up. I've always wondered what his face looked like when Grandma struck Uncle Lane. I meant to ask years ago. Like John and Wendy, neither of those three are here to ask.

Only Mama and myself saw the end of World War Two, Mama from the farmhouse, me from the South Pacific. Wendy and John had passed before the war ever began.

#

Which is what I've been trying to get to this whole time. I've eaten the skin and flesh of the apple and now I've come to the core. I feel just as sick as John did, hollering "Seeds and all, seeds and all." I guess everyone has to take a bite out of the core eventually.

In February of 1938, John and Wendy went ice skating. They'd spent most of the winter trying to make a pair of skates for each of them. Nothing fancy, just a sharpened blade and leather straps that wrapped around a foot. I could tell Pa and Uncle Lane were mighty proud of the kids for sticking to the project and making the best skates they could make. We all offered to go with them that first time. I hoped to get a chuckle at them falling; the adults wanted to keep an eye on safety.

John and Wendy wouldn't have any of it. They told us where they would be and when they'd be home. If I'd told Pa something like that, I'd been on the wrong end of a willow switch. Not Wendy and John; as long as they were together, there wasn't a problem. And they were always together.

Mama sent me out to check on them an hour before they said they'd return. Mama knew when something wasn't right with the children she'd raised. I found the spot they were supposed to be at. I didn't see either of them skating. Must have worn themselves out.

I glimpsed them on the other side of the pond. They were holding each other tight as could be, shivering like frightened squirrels. What wasn't frozen dripped and puddled around them. Mama was right, something happened. Wendy could only stutter, and John couldn't say anything at all. I picked them up and on my shoulders, getting my heavy coat wet for my efforts. I worried the whole walk home that I would stumble and break a leg. I lost track of time.

What seemed like months later, I saw Uncle Lane and Pa running towards me. Pa took John and draped him over his shoulder just as I had done. Uncle Lane cradled Wendy in his arms like a baby. If he started crying now the tears would freeze to his face.

"Can you still walk, son?" Pa said. I was cold and tired, but I could make it home. I nodded yes, and we started walking.

Grandma and Mama were waiting at the door with blankets. They wrapped me up then followed the men into the room John and Wendy shared. I sat by the fire, fearing the worst. I wasn't outside as long as they had been. My walk, although strenuous, could not equal the exuberance I imagined John and Wendy had while skating. Sweating in the cold is a horrible thing.

Uncle Lane came out for hot water. He told me both children looked dreadfully sick. No frostbite, thank goodness, but definitely sick. Pa would go into town to fetch Doctor Peacock. Either way, the kids would be in bed for a length of time.

Doctor Peacock's guess at how long John and Wendy would be in bed differed greatly from Pa's. The Doctor said they wouldn't be in bed much longer at all. At first listen, Pa and Uncle Lane got huge grins on their faces. I knew otherwise. The kids would be out of those beds sooner than Sunday. Not to play, not to laugh and smile and be happy together.

#

We buried them next to each other. Matching caskets, matching headstones. Only differences were the first names and birthdays. And one other thing. John held on as long as he could, but this time he went first. He passed away at 11:30 on March 2, 1938. Uncle Lane held Wendy close to him for another three hours until she slipped away, too. Her last words were "Seeds and all, John, seeds and all."

Let the Devil Take Tomorrow

Remember that time I tried to write a story in which no one died? It didn't work out that first time. "Let the Devil Take Tomorrow" was my second try and technically no one dies within the course of the story. There are dead people, dying people, and references to the ways in which some people will die in the future, but as far as anyone dying on the page . . . not a one.

It wasn't as easy as it sounds. This is a vampire story, which made my goal doubly difficult.

This is also a Las Vegas story, which is one of my favorite kinds. I have a love/hate relationship with Sin City. I went to school there for a couple years and loved it, but the heat . . .dear God. When overnight lows are in the 90s, it's time to go.

Fitzgerald's is gone from Fremont Street, which makes me sad. Sure, it was a dive during its last few years, but there was a bartender there who made the world's best 99-cent margaritas.

The title comes from the Kris Kristofferson-penned song "Help Me Make it Through the Night." It's perhaps the most vampiric country song ever recorded. (Also, I freaking hate "Don't Stop Believin'" by Journey. It should be banned from karaoke everywhere.)

The host's pointed nail scratched down the list, looking

for one song he could bear.

"My friends and I really want to do that 'Believing' song," the girl in the tight pink UNLV tank top said. "It's Megan's 21-run and that is totally our song."

He reached the end of the list, passing over four other requests for "Don't Stop Believin'" and jotted *Megan and friends-DSB* in his calligraphy-like style on an empty line.

"I'll see if I can squeeze you in sooner," he said. He smiled—the casino owners paid him to smile—but not wide enough to show his teeth. Tank top girl's jugular, exposed thanks to the plunging neckline of her top, pulsed for everyone to see, not just him, and her naked arms held light blue veins begging to be used like straws to her heart.

"Thank you, thankyouthankyou," she said, jumping spryly into the air. "We'll be over there." She waved at a table of four other girls, equally defrocked, one of whom wore a cheap plastic crown with a fake purple gem to match her own Runnin' Rebels tank top. The four girls waved back, all smiles and flesh. The host waved, too, just a simple gesture to assure the young women that he would do his part to make their night a success and good tips be damned.

Oh, how he longed for the simpler nights when he could secure work as a Black Jack or baccarat dealer without a pesky background check. Fingerprinting had become more sophisticated, identification cards more complex, and soon he had been forced to seek alternate employment. But he could not say goodbye to his beloved Las Vegas. The gambling halls had shunned him—if they only knew the truth—yet he could not turn his four-and-a-half hundred-year-old back on his precious desert jewel. His crisp, white shirts were dingier than they once were, and his current employers encouraged him to branch out and don more colorful bow ties than the traditional black he preferred, but still he stayed.

A single *beep* from his wristwatch informed him the time had come to begin the night's festivities.

"Welcome to Carnahan's Karaoke at Fitzgerald's on Fremont Street," the host cooed into the microphone. He had spent years learning to modulate his own voice for the electronic amplifiers. He didn't need the microphone; he could make himself heard as far away as the Luxor on the far end of the Strip, if he so desired. For these tourists and local thrill seekers, however, the host needed to pull back and not blow their eardrums out.

Not even just for fun.

The Friday night crowd applauded, more for themselves than him, he knew. These people were the stars of the evening, all ready to be three-minute idols.

"We have a live mic and live audience," he said, enjoying his own joke. "Let us begin."

He swirled around, the bottom of his purple velvet jacket floating out like a poor substitute for the old black leather cape he wore before Nevada—before the United States, even—existed. Halfway through his turn, he flashed the list of potential talent, a white flurry that reflected Fitzgerald's green and gold neon. A wave of applause pressed against him and he stopped, straightened his jacket, and smoothed the list. He didn't need to look at the piece of paper. He could see the aroused anticipation and smell the vodka sweat of the middle-aged man at the table nearest the small stage.

"Jerry, you're up," the host said to the nervous man before addressing the audience. "Ladies and gentlemen, Gerald Bivins."

As Jerry mounted the stage, taking the microphone, the host caught a glimpse of the woman Jerry would be singing for and had been singing for since Carnahan's Karaoke started two years prior: a waitress from the buffet downstairs, in the middle of her age just as Jerry. Her graying hair did not impress the host, nor did her walk, which reminded him of the deteriorating state of the very casino at which she and the host were both employed. Jerry's desire for the waitress, however, rolled off him on the crests of White Russians and gave the host enough energy to survive Jerry's singing.

Jerry, the host had learned, was not born in south Detroit. Once, about six months ago, Jerry had wanted to preface his Journey by stating he'd grown up on an island off the coast of Washington state. The host caught the thought and pushed back, mentally helping Jerry skip to the song and avoid telling the audience the story of how he went from being a nobody on an island that sounded like snakes to a divorced nobody in Vegas. Nor was the object of Jerry's desire a small-town girl. She was from Parnassus, New Jersey, and had worked at the casino since it opened as the Sundance Hotel in 1980. Her hometown was blazoned on the gold name tag she wore below "Brenda" and above "27 years."

The host stood off-stage and watched two couples leave their tables. *They must have stopped believing,* he thought and crossed two names off his list.

"That was for you, Brenda," Jerry said as he finished his song. The host appeared beside him and took the microphone before he could drop it on the floor.

"Thank you, Jerry. We will let Brenda know," said the host. The audience clapped and Jerry took his seat. He wiped a mask of sweat from his brow and swallowed the remnants of the White Russian he had left behind before his performance. The host watched Jerry as the liquid ran down the man's throat to his stomach. Only a scant few hours had passed since the host awoke for the night and consumed a pint from his own stock, yet his hunger crept up on him now.

He shifted his eyes to the table of college girls and was tempted to allow them to have their turn just to be rid of fake Steven Perrys for the night. Taking singers out of order, however, was against the house rules. Breaking the rules—like broken fingers and noses, which heal eventually—brought more attention to the host than he cared to deal with. And so he called forth the next performers.

An elderly couple took the stage and the host produced a second microphone. Janice and Ian, like Jerry, were regulars of Carnahan's Karaoke, singing the same song together once a week probably even before the vampire began hosting this sing-along spectacular at Fitzgerald's. As Ian spoke the first lines of "Jackson," the host saw the fever that had first joined the couple together forty years before. The host saw Ian as he had been: leather jacket, knee-high boots, and Indian motorcycle rumbling up to young Janice's front walk. Janice, barely eighteen, carried a small bag down the steps and strapped onto the back of the bike before taking the helmet the twenty-one-year-old Ian had purchased for her. Her parents did not follow Janice out the door that day but watched from the living room windows. They expected she would return alone or perhaps with a baby someday, but she never did.

The host relived this story every week and every week he cried. No great love had ever come his way, although he had lived through scores of plague and fever. He could not have saved Mathilda from typhoid fever, and Sebastian had succumbed to yellow fever. Plagues of one sort or another had always taken his lovers.

When Janice and Ian finished, the host assisted them back to their table. "A round for the Elmwoods," he exclaimed, catching the attention of a passing cocktail waitress.

"Thank you, dear," Janice said, planting a kiss on the host's cheek and a fifty-dollar bill in his palm. He could feel the difference in this currency from the usual ten or occasional twenty the Elmwoods tipped him. He probed deeper than he liked to do and saw medical reports, doctors' recommendations, and a last will and testament signed by Janice. The host hesitated, but then shook Ian's hand and saw a rope and a gun and he quickly let go.

The host returned to his stage and scanned the crowd again. The young woman who had taken the final spot on the night's list giggled with her friends over tequila shots and cheap champagne. These women were born during a boom for Las Vegas but had started to come of age first during the city's appeal to families and now during the bust. The host had seen all manner of famine during his time and wished he could show these tarts what true need and starvation were like. Instead, he motioned to another young woman and beckoned her to the stage.

The petite woman stood and maneuvered her way past three tables. The eyes of a few men followed her, trying to plumb the secrets beneath the burgundy smock dress she wore. Her lithe frame was topped by a bespectacled face and closely-cropped dark hair.

"Pamela," he smiled. "Welcome."

"Sure," she said as she reached out to take his hand held out in assistance. Her fingers snapped back at his cold touch, but he smiled his most reassuring smile and she reached out again. She returned the host's smile and he knew she would be the star of the evening.

Even if he had to help.

Pamela held the microphone against her curled lips and faced the screen behind her as the blue letters began scrolling lyrics for her. Her shy warble of the first words, *Lo-ong ago, and so fa-ar … away*, barely reached the middle tables. Eyes that had tracked her movements wandered. Ears stretched for snippets of other conversations. Pamela was losing her audience, which meant it was time for the real show to begin.

The host caught Pamela's hooded eyes with his own laser-like gaze. She had only reached the first chorus and he did not want her to fail so soon. He forced images of grandiose women, commanding the attention of all around them, into Pamela's mind: Helen of Troy, Cleopatra of Egypt, Joan of Arc, and Diana of Themyscira. He altered the images so that Pamela would see herself as each of these bold women: sword drawn when need be, deadly beautiful when called for.

She turned away from the screen and the host followed, never allowing his eyes to break from hers. She tugged the microphone away from her lips, widened her stature, and raised her other hand in front of her. As the second chorus appeared in blue, the host turned off the sound system and used a trick his master had taught him to amplify Pamela's voice through himself and across the casino floor. A smattering of Fremont Street passersby stopped at the open doors to listen to Pamela's rising voice.

"Don't you remember you told me you loved me, ba-aby." Pamela sang, and each syllable hung in the air like a floating diamond. She strutted across the small stage, never again looking at the words scrolling by on the screen. As her lungs filled with invigorating air, her chest strained against her dress and a small tear formed at the knee of her stockings.

The host dodged the assault of lewd thoughts from many of the men and some of the women—a particularly vivid image of Megan's plastic crown dangling from Pamela's foot threatened to overtake him—and a handful of caring and caressing thoughts about Pamela. Once, and not so long ago as it seemed, he would have preferred the lust and carnal desires he absorbed from his audiences. But now, after far too many lost loves with no path to release for himself such as Ian had chosen, the host preferred a purer love, one more difficult to obtain. He would take what he could get, however, even if only for one night.

Flushed and exhausted, Pamela left the stage. The host mouthed the word *superstar* to her and he smiled again. He saw her refuse numerous offers of drinks, business cards, hotel keys, and open seats as she returned to her own table. A fresh Long Island Iced Tea awaited her there. She sipped sensuously and any remaining tension slipped away from her body. *Tomorrow*, the host thought, *she may be a shy and appeasing mouse again or she may begin to roar.* But that would be tomorrow; tonight had not yet reached a conclusion.

The host sentried a selection of rock ballads, Megan and friends' rendition of "Don't Stop Believin'" during which Megan's eyes never veered away from Pamela, and one above average "Luck Be a Lady," after which he was ready to close the festivities for another night.

"Thank you, all, for joining us at Carnahan's Karaoke, and at Fitzgerald's," he said. He continued his spiel, just as he had done every week for two years. The cadences were familiar: they were the same as those he used dealing cards before the world became a digital playground, and the same as his speeches to politicians before the frontier was conquered. He had not rehearsed even as an actor in London when he'd been a young night owl of barely one hundred. All those nights, so many alone, so few with a heartbeat that lasted into the morning.

He wrapped his hands around the microphone and his song queued in the machine without him needing to touch it. Las Vegas had given him Elvis and Tom Jones, but the host had found himself drawn more to America's musical outlaws. He had once convinced Janice and Ian to sing "Folsom Prison Blues" with him around the time of the Man in Black's death. He would sing lines such as "They buried me in that great tomb, but I am still around" without a hint of irony.

Tonight the host needed help. He needed help to make it through the night, so he turned to Willie Nelson's voice and Kris Kristofferson's words to show his audience how he felt. His pointed fingernails clacked against each other as he trilled through the first lines and into the heart of the song, its early morning light trying to reach his dark heart.

He saw Ian drape his withered arm around Janice's shoulders, and she leaned into him. The host tried not to see the pulsing clumps of renegade blackness in her lungs or the walnut of unfamiliar tissue inside Pamela's head. He avoided the bleeding shadow inside Jerry's liver and shut off all images inside his head after a sweeping of red and blue lights, darkened tank tops, and a shattered crown fought for space in his brain. He sang louder, about bygone days and nights so long he wished for nothing more than a friend.

The host, who so many members of his audience called Carnahan and whose parents had called Dedo, found the nasal tone of his idol but filled it with yearning beyond the years of the Texas-bred singer. He yearned for the lives of his audience to fill him. For the blood to pour from femoral arteries, brachials, and carotids. But he yearned also for them to live. He could not end the suffering of Janice nor prevent the demise of Ian. He might perhaps be able to pluck the burgeoning tumor from Pamela's brain, but doing so would not leave her unharmed. Jerry would live for years before the cirrhosis turned him yellow.

And as for Megan and her young friends, well, he could help them avoid the traffic between Fremont Street and their dorms on Tropicana Avenue, but doing so would not keep them alive.

He focused his energy on the final two lines of the last verse.

Let the devil take tomorrow...

He smiled his deepest smile of the night and maybe some of his audience saw the fangs he'd hidden so well for so many years.

Lord, tonight I need a friend...

All of his yesterdays were dead and gone and had been for centuries. And he knew that for him tomorrow was indeed out of sight. But tomorrow offered another night at Carnahan's; he just needed a friend to help him make it through one more night.

Scream Queen

"Scream Queen" was written around the same time as "Hath No Fury" but is rooted in influences older to me than Tarantino. It's a Stephen King story with no apologies. Like "An Appointment with the Knifeman," it could have slithered off the pages of EC Comics and become an episode of "Tales From the Crypt."

If you don't like foul-mouthed teenagers, this isn't for you. If you liked "Stranger Things," the 2016 Netflix series or are eagerly awaiting the theatrical remake of IT, *this story is for you, although much less heart-warming in its nostalgia. And if you read* Cry Down Dark, *my novel from 2016, you'll recognize parts of this as having been written by that book's hero, Peter Toombs. If you like it, great. If you don't, blame him.*

Maybe that's why God made us kids first and built us close to the ground, because He knows you got to fall down a lot and bleed a lot before you learn that one simple lesson. You pay for what you get, you own what you pay for . . . and sooner or later whatever you own comes back home to you.

IT by Stephen King

He couldn't have been the only person to hear her screaming. Other boys and girls were playing in the streets and in their yards. Four dogs of various sizes barked at equal volumes. So why, J.D. wondered, was he the only one to hear the screaming?

J.D. had moved to Springvale three months before his fourteenth birthday. The first two months were filled with the usual "new kid" grievances. J.D. didn't mind. It didn't bother him that some of the other kids caught him reading *Dracula* and decided to make fun of him for it.

"At least I can read," he told the group huddled around him. Throughout the attempted taunting, J.D. never looked up. He didn't look up when he heard another voice coming to his defense.

"Leave him alone, you assholes," the voice said. It was a girl's voice, one that J.D. almost recognized. "He didn't do anything to you."

The temptation to raise his head grew. Still, J.D. kept his nose in the book. Seeing that J.D. wasn't going to take the bait, the crowd thinned then disappeared. When he thought it was safe, J.D. closed the book and looked up. He didn't see anyone. Not even the girl who likely saved him from his first beating in the new school.

That night he heard the screams for the first time. He rolled over in bed, assuming someone had their TV on too loud.

J.D. was in the library the next time he heard the voice. He was looking over the school's sparse selection of Stephen King books, all of which he'd read and only a couple he didn't own.

"These are here mostly for the staff," he heard the girl say.

"What?" J.D. said.

"The Stephen King books. No one but the staff reads them. And me, I guess. My name is Alice. You're J.D., right?"

"Uh, yeah."

"Sorry about the other day. Some of the kids here are real jerks. Sometimes I wish I could just go apeshit on them, like *Carrie*."

"Carrie dies in the end."

"Yeah, but she takes enough assholes with her to make it worth it. Did you know the library doesn't even have *The Stand*?"

"Really? They should at least have that."

"And the parents won't let them buy a copy of *It*. They don't want us reading about bad things happening to kids, I guess."

J.D. ran a finger along the spine of *Pet Sematary*. "Have you read *It*?"

"No."

"Well, believe me, it isn't just the bad things they don't want you to read."

"What is it then?"

"I'll lend you my copy and you can tell me."

"OK." Alice put her hand out and J.D. shook it. Alice's hand was soft, like a girl's should be, but J.D. could feel calluses on her fingertips. She must play guitar, J.D. thought.

"Look," Alice continued, casually letting go of J.D.'s hand. "I have to get going. Meet me here tomorrow?"

"Same Bat-time..." J.D. started.

"Same Bat-channel," Alice finished. J.D. watched her walk out of the library, noticing all three times she looked back at him.

Wow, he thought. A girl talked to me. And she likes Stephen King. Don't forget to bring the book. Don't forget. Don't forget.

#

J.D. forgot. He spent all night in a daze. He didn't do

his homework, and he barely touched his dinner. Even though he hadn't ever kissed a girl yet, he dreamed of making out with Alice at the Springvale gazebo. He could have let the dream go on forever except that, in the background, he could hear someone screaming.

It was while he was replaying the dream that J.D. remembered he was supposed to bring his copy of *It* for Alice. He raised his hand, hoping to get Mrs. Jaworski's attention.

"Yes, Mr. Sable. A question?" she said.

"No, Mrs. Jaworski. I need to go. I have an appointment." The lie might come back on him, but he had to chance it.

"Do you have a note?" Mrs. Jaworski asked.

"I left it in my locker."

"Very well. Make sure you bring me that note tomorrow. Otherwise, I will have to mark you for an unexcused absence."

"Thank you, Mrs. Jaworski," J.D. said as he gathered his books and rushed out of the classroom.

He couldn't go home. His mom was there. Even if he could get in without her noticing, he couldn't get by his dog, Krueger. There was no way he could get the book for Alice. He was going to blow his best shot at a new friend, possibly a girlfriend. There must be another way. There must be a...

At the end of the block was a Rite-Aid. Many of J.D.'s paperbacks had been purchased at just such a place. He held his head high, trying to look as old as he could. He walked by the front counter, heading to the direction of the book and magazine section. This is easier than I thought, J.D. told himself.

"Sir," someone said from behind him.

Shit, J.D. thought. *I'm busted*. He turned around and faced the Rite-Aid manager.

"Sir, you need to leave your bag at the front counter.

You can pick it up when you leave."

Relief washed over J.D. He wasn't busted. J.D. followed the vested gentleman to the counter and placed his bag on the clerk side of the counter. He then turned back to his original destination.

Under the heading "Popular Authors," J.D. found the shelf with Stephen King books. At first glance, the shelf seemed better stocked than the library. J.D. soon realized this was due to multiple copies of the same titles. He also saw that none of them were *It*.

J.D. flipped through copies of *Misery*, *The Dark Half*, and *Night Shift*. Finally, behind four copies of *Cujo*, was the Rite-Aid's only copy of *It*.

"Thank you," J.D. said out loud. A woman looking at romance novels glared at him. J.D. returned her stare with a smile.

"Your parents let you read such trash," the woman said, still looking at her Harlequins.

"No offense, ma'am," J.D. said, "but I'd be more worried about your own reading tastes." He walked away before she could say anything else. Besides, J.D. didn't want to take up any more of her time, seeing as how she was probably on her way to a Lonely Housewives Club meeting. I bet she is top bitch, too, J.D. thought.

J.D. paid for his purchase, grabbed his bag and nearly started home. He still couldn't go home; school wouldn't let out for another two hours. Besides, his date—Date? Could he call it that?—was at the school library. If he went back to school now, they'd know he skipped out. J.D. decided to visit the site of the dream: the gazebo. It was only a couple blocks away. He could sit there and read until it was time to meet Alice.

He set the alarm on his wristwatch and sat down in the gazebo. Sitting on the wooden bench was like sitting on a million splinters. J.D. wondered how anyone, even dream people, could make out sitting there. He took out a comic book and tried reading. He barely made it beyond the splash page; all his thoughts went back to Alice.

J.D. wondered if her calluses were from an acoustic guitar or an electric one. He wondered what Stephen King book Alice read first and which was her favorite. He wondered if she would ask him the same questions. J.D. opened the new copy of *It* and took out his pen. After scribbling on the title page he put the book back in its sack.

J.D. must have been drifting longer than he thought. Shortly after replacing the book, his alarm went off. J.D corralled his thoughts and gathered his things. He made it back to school in mere minutes. He made sure to avoid the halls where he knew he might be recognized. He made it safely to the library and walked straight to the K section. He saw Alice, flippantly turning the pages of *The Dead Zone*.

When she turned around, J.D. knew he was falling in love. The black T-shirt Alice wore had dark red writing on it. The words "All Hail The Crimson King" were written below a sketched eye of the same color.

"Do you like my shirt?" Alice asked.

"Um, yeah. Where'd you get it?" J.D. tried not to mumble, and so far he was doing OK. He knew it was only a matter of time before he said something stupid.

"I made it. Here." Alice bent over, reaching into her own backpack. She pulled out an identical T-shirt to the one she had on, only larger. "I made you one, also." She tossed the shirt at J.D. He dropped his bag in order to catch it. Without really thinking, he slipped the shirt over his head and pulled it down to cover the shirt he already had on.

"Thanks. I love it. I have something for you, too." J.D. thanked fate that he'd forgotten his own copy of *It* and was forced to buy a new copy for Alice. He pulled out the book and handed it to her.

"For your own copy, it doesn't look like you've read it

very often," she said, a hint of worry in her voice.

"Truth is, I only opened this once. I thought you might like to have your own copy." J.D. tried to look as innocent as he could, hoping she wouldn't refuse the gift.

"Are you sure? I mean, it isn't like you knew I'd give you something. You did this for me?" Alice still sounded worried, like she was in a dream of her own and she might wake up any second.

"Yeah I'm sure. Here, let me show you something." J.D. moved to stand next to Alice and opened the book. He turned to the title page. There his quick inscription stood out, the ink not entirely dry.

> *To my new friend Alice,*
> *This is a book about friends and*
> *how having a friend can save your life.*
> *I hope you like* IT,
> *Your Friend,*
> *J.D. Sable*

J.D. read the inscription out loud. When he finished, Alice turned and hugged him, flattening the book and J.D.'s hands between them. Stunned, J.D. wasn't sure if he should hug back. The book was still in his hands, sandwiched between them. He didn't know what Alice would do if he moved his hands, so he left them where they were.

Alice released J.D. from the hug but did not stop smiling. "Thank you, J.D.," she said. "This means so much."

"You're welcome." J.D. couldn't help but smile, too. Being that close to Alice, having his hands where they were, had excited J.D. more than he at first realized. He hoped Alice hadn't noticed.

"I have an idea," Alice said, taking her new book in one hand and J.D.'s hand in her other. "Let's go to the gazebo. We can read to each other."

J.D. laughed. Of course she would want to go to the gazebo, the setting of his make out dream and ultimate place to waste time. "Sure," he said. "The gazebo sounds great."

Ever the young gentleman, J.D. hoisted both of their bags on one of his shoulders. His other hand was still caught in the grip of Alice's hand. It didn't take long for his palm to begin sweating. Just another thing J.D. hoped Alice wouldn't notice.

They left the library but not fast enough. The taunts began before Alice and J.D. reached the doors to freedom.

"Hey, look. Two freaks holding hands. Look everybody! They're gonna go make freak babies."

J.D. wanted to keep walking. He tugged Alice's hand, hoping she'd ignore the teasing. Alice, however, stopped cold. She didn't let go of J.D.'s sweaty hand, but she did turn to face the small mob.

"Listen, you fucking dickheads," Alice began. Her face, previously blushing, turned a deeper red. Angry red. "If you don't leave us alone, I'll come to all your houses and cut you up into little pieces. Then I'll stuff those pieces up your mommies' pussies until they spill out their cocksucking mouths."

J.D. had never heard a girl talk like that and, from the looks of the faces in the crowd, neither had they. He was impressed and scared. A few boys in the crowd immediately backed off, but one of them (J.D. recalled his voice from the *Dracula* day) stepped up to stare Alice in the face.

"I'd like to see you try it, whore," he said. The strain on his face nearly popped a few of the pimples peppering his cheeks and forehead. "The only thing you know about cocksucking is how to do it. I bet you don't even do it right."

"You'd be the one to know, Gary," Alice said, meeting the challenge head on. "I bet your faggot brother taught you the right way."

Gary, like many schoolyard bullies, stepped back before

taking his first swing at Alice. She ducked and pushed J.D. out of the way simultaneously. Gary's second attempt at a punch came in lower. Alice kicked him in the wrist hard enough to force Gary's fist into his own mouth. J.D. stood back, waiting to see what would happen. Alice still held her book in one hand. She wiped sweat from her brow and pushed a newly out of place strand of hair behind her ear.

"What's the matter, Gary," someone from the crowd yelled. "Can't you hit a girl?"

Gary turned his back on Alice and shouted into the thinning crowd. "Who said that? Who fucking said that?"

With his back turned, Alice took the opportunity to kick Gary in the ass. He went sprawling face first into the dirty hall floor. Alice seized J.D.'s hand and the two of them ran out the doors before Gary could regain his feet.

#

"I really don't know what came over me," Alice said as they reached the gazebo. "I guess I lost control."

J.D. didn't buy that. To him, Alice seemed to be in complete control. She saved him (again) and embarrassed Gary. The entire time—not that it was very long; schoolyard fights rarely last more than a few seconds—she never let go of the book J.D. bought her.

They sat down on the mass of splinters J.D. had only recently vacated. Alice scooted herself as close to J.D. as she could get. Although it made him slightly uncomfortable being this close to a girl he now knew could kick his ass, the discomfort was balanced by the knowledge that Alice likely wouldn't kick his ass.

"You were great, Alice," J.D. said. "I mean, I thought Gary would back off after what you said, but you were ready. You knew he'd try to hit you, didn't you?"

"Yeah, well, he's tried shit like that before. Sometimes worse. Usually I just walk away. But I didn't want him to ruin our shirts. Or this book. I'll cherish it forever."

There was a moment between them when J.D. thought about leaning over to kiss Alice on the cheek. Just as he turned his head to do it, Alice's lips touched his. He jerked his head back, not because he didn't like it but because he wasn't exactly sure what happened.

"I'm sorry, J.D.," Alice said. "I meant to kiss your cheek but you…"

"Yeah, I was going to…to…" J.D. had been waiting to say something stupid. That was a definite start. "I've never kissed a girl before."

"Do you want to try again?" Alice asked.

"Should we? I mean, I…" J.D. didn't finish his sentence. With his mouth hanging open, Alice kissed him again. He didn't dare move his head. Alice leaned further into him, putting one hand on his leg and the other on his shoulder, that hand still holding the book. J.D. let himself be kissed, afraid that anything he did would ruin the moment.

This is just like my dream, he thought. The he remembered the rest of the dream. The awful screaming in the background. He broke the kiss and looked into Alice's hazel eyes.

"What's wrong, J.D.?" Alice asked him. "You look like a skeleton just grabbed your ankle."

"I'm fine. I just remembered this dream I had."

"Did you dream we were kissing in the gazebo?"

"Yes. I did."

"Me too."

"No, you didn't. That's too weird."

"I did. Why do you think I wanted to come here?" Alice said, taking hold of J.D.'s hand again. "I wanted to see if dreams come true."

"I guess they do." J.D. initiated their next kiss. Both of

them hoped it would not be their last.

#

J.D. walked Alice home, discovering that her house was only four doors down and across the street from his own house.

"Hey, Alice, did you know I live just up the block?" J.D. asked, still holding her hand.

"Yeah, I did. I watched you move in."

"What?"

"I watched you move in. I mean, we haven't had a new family on the street for a long time. I was curious."

"But you didn't come say hi?"

"I couldn't say hello to a stranger. Like, what if you were a serial killer or something?"

"You don't know that I'm not."

"Yes, I do. I know them when I see them." Alice winked and kissed J.D. again, first on the cheek then the lips. "I have to go. My dad will be wondering where I've been."

"Yeah, mine too," J.D. said. He wanted the night to last forever. Alice's hand slipped from his. Never once did she complain about his sweaty palm. She never said he was a bad kisser, either.

"Goodnight, J.D. See you tomorrow," Alice said, opening her front door and walking through it.

"Goodnight, Alice," J.D. said. He smiled the whole way home. Not that it was very far.

The smile lasted through the night. J.D. couldn't remember what he dreamt but he knew it was good.

When J.D. left his house the next morning, Alice was at the curb, waiting for him. She had on a RAMONES T-shirt and ripped jeans. To J.D. she might as well have been wearing white robes and a halo; she was so beautiful. Like his own horror-punk goddess. His scream queen.

"What?" Alice said, softly punching J.D. in the arm. "You look like you are about to explode."

"I just…It's…" J.D. took a deep breath before trying to say anything else. "I like your shirt."

"Of course you do." She turned around and pointed to her back. "Check that out." Emblazoned on the shirt were the words "Rocket To Russia Tour" and a list of cities and dates.

"Holy shit," J.D. said. "Is this real or a replica?"

"It's real. My mom and dad met at the show. Dad always said that Mom could drive him wild in this shirt. Figured it'd work for me, too. Is it working, J.D.?" Alice shimmied her still-developing hips and breasts at J.D.

"Yes, it's working. Now stop it before my mom sees you."

"C'mon, let's go." Alice reached out for J.D.'s hand, the same hand that lost about five gallons of sweat the previous afternoon.

"I didn't think anyone could be so excited about going to school," said J.D.

"You're silly. We aren't going to school," Alice said. She pulled him off the curb and headed in the general direction of the school. From experience, J.D. knew you could get to plenty of places walking this direction, not just school.

"Aren't you going to ask where we're going?" Alice asked.

"No, I'm not. I want to be surprised," J.D. replied.

"Ooh, this is new. A man that doesn't want to be in control. I could learn to like this." Alice kissed him again. J.D. already liked that.

They didn't end up at the gazebo like J.D. thought they would. Not that he minded; any more making out and J.D.'s pants would burst. All this was new to him. That other thing —the thing he really wanted to do but was also scared to death of doing—might happen sooner than he thought. At thirteen, J.D. wasn't afraid of dying a virgin. He simply expected to be driving before his first time.

Instead of the gazebo, the teens found themselves in a wooded area near the edge of town. J.D. had never been there, but it didn't take long for anyone to hear about the Forest. For much of Springvale's history, the Forest was the place high school kids came to get drunk, stoned, or laid.

Then, a year ago—or longer, depending on who you heard it from—the body of a sixteen-year-old girl was found out there. Bits of crime scene tape, faded, still clung to a few trees and bushes. Despite the books and movies J.D. had consumed, he felt scared. He knew that teens who have sex in the forest get killed, whether by machete, axe, or chainsaw. Dead is dead. J.D. did not want to be dead.

"J.D., hey, what's wrong?"

"Nothing. Just thinking."

"You're thinking about Stacy Handel, aren't you?"

"Who's that?"

"The girl that got killed out here. Don't worry. That slut deserved what happened to her. If she decides to come a-haunting, I'll kick her ass just like I kicked Gary's." That angry red color started creeping up Alice's face. She squeezed J.D.'s hand like she wanted to tear it off.

"Alice, hey, c'mon. I didn't even know her. Calm down, please."

For a moment, J.D. was absolutely sure that was the stupidest thing he'd ever said. Not just stupid enough to get him punched out but stupid enough to get him killed. He had no doubt that Alice could kill him, if she wanted to.

Alice let go of J.D.'s hand, smiled, and sat down on the ground. "Oh, J.D.," she said, the red fading from her cheeks. "You don't need to worry about anything. That skank is long gone."

J.D. wondered exactly what Alice had against the deceased Stacy Handel. He made a conscious effort to put it out of his mind and focus on the possibilities for this ditch day with Alice.

Alice, after her brief tirade, stretched her young body flat on the ground. She made her body into a single line, arms reaching for the crest of a small hill and toes pointing at J.D. Much like that first hug in the library and first kiss at the gazebo, this sight awoke a fresh burst of adolescent yearning in J.D. He stood there, unable to move, transfixed as if he were watching a video of the first Playmate to walk on the moon.

"You know," Alice said, "you can lie down next to me."

While not completely out of this trance-like state, J.D. was able to take a few steps then maneuver himself onto the ground. He sat on a rock, but instead of standing back up he reached under his butt and took hold of the rock. He threw it, not caring where it went. The rock bounced off a tree a few feet away.

"Nice shot," Alice said.

"Five-time American League All-Star from the Boston Red Sox, J.D. Sable," he called out as he relaxed his body next to Alice's.

"You aren't bitter about being traded from the team mere months before they won the Series, are you?" Alice asked, now teasing him.

"Thanks for reminding me." J.D. turned on his side, faking mad. Alice turned also and draped her arm over J.D.'s shoulder.

"Would a hug make my little All-Star feel better?" she asked, her voice somewhere between motherly and lusty.

J.D. switched sides, now facing Alice. He raised one arm, and Alice slid into place, pressing her body against J.D.'s. He wrapped his arms around her, slipping one hand beneath her. Alice snuggled up to him, placing her head on his shoulder.

With smiles on both their faces, the kids—a little more

grown up now—stayed like that until they fell asleep. Neither said a word.

#

J.D. thought the screaming was just a part of the dream. Then he started hearing words in the scream. "No, Daddy, no," and "I'm your good girl," were the closest things to whole sentences. Other words, like "hurts," "stop," "kill," and a thousand "no's" assaulted J.D.'s slumbering mind.

Small fists hitting J.D. in the chest fully awoke him. Alice was pummeling him, trying to struggle out of the circle his arms made around her. Her eyes were still closed but her mouth alternated between a grimace of pain and the megaphone for the screams responsible for ending J.D.'s dream.

Rolling over, J.D. grabbed Alice's shoulders and shook her. "Alice, Alice!" J.D. said, nearly screaming himself. "Alice, what's wrong?"

Alice opened her eyes and looked through J.D. The eyes J.D. had almost fallen into were straining and damp with tears. "It hurts. It hurts. I'm a good girl. I don't want it to hurt anymore." She spoke, flinging the words at J.D. but not to him.

"Alice," J.D. said, trying to sound soothing despite his our fear. "What hurts? I didn't hurt you, did I?"

She closed her eyes, opened them, and then blinked again. She looked at J.D., seeing him for the first time since waking up. "Oh, J.D., I had the worst nightmare. Please, let's just forget it." She put her arms around him, not the embrace of a lover but of a scared child hoping to be comforted.

As much as J.D. wanted to forget how Alice woke up— and woke him up—he couldn't. He knew who'd been screaming all those nights.

After not looking at each other or saying anything for

half an hour, Alice stood up and put her hand on J.D.'s head. "Follow me," she said. "I have something I need to show you."

They walked farther into the Forest and soon reached a clearing surrounded by tall trees. Even at mid-day the trees blocked out most of the sunlight. J.D. lost the trail they'd walked to get there. He didn't think it possible to experience claustrophobia outdoors, but this place showed him he was wrong.

Alice stopped in the middle of the clearing, leaving J.D. a few feet behind. She shivered in the evening-like dimness and crossed her arms. She scanned the clearing, her eyes never settling on one spot. J.D. tried to ask her what was going on, but Alice quickly shushed him.

Alice, looking above them at the sun they could barely see, spoke.

"After my mom died, Daddy and I would come here for picnics. He liked it because no one could see us. We'd have late lunches and early dinners by candlelight and still be home before bedtime. We were supposed to have a picnic that afternoon but I got detention. When I made it home, Daddy wasn't here and all the picnic stuff was gone.

"I thought he'd left without me but that he'd wait to eat until I could meet him at our spot. I ran the whole way. When I got here, I saw her on top of him. That's what I remember most. She was on top of him and they were on our picnic blanket. Her clothes were thrown all over and Daddy's were folded and sitting on top of the picnic basket."

At first, J.D. didn't know who Alice was talking about. As he listened to her, it didn't take much longer for him to catch on.

"That skank. She was using my picnic time. My special time with Daddy. They didn't hear me. Daddy was grunting like a pig and she was saying things I'd never heard.

"She kept saying horrible things like she was his little

girl, not me. I screamed. I couldn't help it. I screamed louder than when Daddy told me Mom was dead.

"They saw me then. She smiled and winked at me. Daddy pushed her off of him and stood up. I could see his thing. He didn't even try to hide it. He picked up his clothes and walked away. The skank just sat there with her tits pointing at the tree tops.

"I wanted to kill her just by staring hate into her, but it didn't work. I used the knife from the picnic basket. Daddy would use it to slice apples. It wasn't very big, so I had to stab her a lot. She bled all over the picnic blanket."

J.D. had backed his way against the wall of trees. As much as he wanted to run, he didn't dare. She knew where he lived.

"I left her there, naked as when I saw her on top of Daddy. I took all the picnic stuff home and burned it. They didn't find her for almost a week.

"I didn't see Daddy until the next afternoon. He hugged me and told me that I really was his good little girl, but that he'd have to punish me. I…I'm not going to tell you what he does."

J.D. had a good idea about what Alice's father had been doing to her. He thought he did, anyway. Alice had stopped talking and started crying. Her sobbing overrode J.D.'s fear, and he went to her. He reached out to her, and she screamed.

That's the scream, J.D. thought. It's been Alice every time. She really is the scream queen.

Alice stopped her wailing and put her arms around J.D.'s neck. "Daddy said if I ever told anyone about what he does to me he'd tell the police I killed Stacy. He says he has some evidence that didn't get burned up.

"You're my only friend, J.D. The only friend I've really had since my mom died. I know about what the kids do in that book. I know you'd never do anything to hurt me. That's why I need your help. I need you to help me stop Daddy from doing bad things to me."

Hand in hand, Alice and J.D. ambled out of the forest. If anyone had been there to see them, they would have thought they were seeing two young lovers not sure of exactly what they'd just done. J.D. knew what he didn't do but wasn't entirely sure of exactly what he did do. He was still trying to accept the silent agreement between himself and Alice. He believed her story, though. Knowing that someone, whether it was her father or not, had been hurting Alice was enough to bring that angry red color to his own face. He squeezed Alice's hand, and she squeezed back. She pecked him on the cheek, and he felt some of the lingering dampness on her face.

J.D., still a month shy of his fourteenth birthday, decided he was in love and would do whatever it took to make sure his true love would never cry again.

#

They went the long way around the block in order to not pass J.D.'s house. There was still a chance of being caught, but the potential consequences were nothing compared to the hell Alice had been going through. Thinking of things that could make a person scream like Alice had back in the Forest both disgusted and enraged J.D.

They could hear the TV when Alice opened the backdoor. Her dad was home, watching a baseball game. I'll bet he's a Yankee fan, J.D. thought. He saw that they were in the kitchen. J.D. remembered that he hadn't had anything to eat since breakfast. Considering what he was about to do, food was not a good idea.

He didn't hear Alice open the drawer, but he recognized the weight and feel of the knife she put in his hand. "Help me, J.D.," Alice whispered in his ear. "Help me not to hurt anymore."

J.D. nodded his head and followed Alice into the living room. He wrapped his hands around the handle of the knife and waited for his scream queen to tell him what to do. If he did it right, maybe he could be her crimson king.

Dead Again Tomorrow

I'm not a poet. Every now and again, I work on something. If I work on a poem long enough, it usually turns out decent. "Dead Again Tomorrow" turned out better than decent and is the only poem I've been paid for.

Rhonda Parrish at "Niteblade" ran this in March 2009, two months after she notified me of acceptance. The day I got the notice was January 19, 2009, the 200th anniversary of the birth of Edgar Allan Poe. If you don't think that's awesome, you might be reading the wrong book.

"It's not death if you refuse it... It is if you accept it."
– James O'Barr

Open your eyes.
      Open…your…eyes.
      OPEN YOUR EYES.

Now, breathe.
      Inhale.
      Exhale.

Do it again. Alive.
    You are alive.
    Can you move your arms?

Good. Find the zipper,
    yes, right there next to your head.
    A shard of jagged light.

Stick your finger through,
    push down.
    Don't want to be stuck

in this bag any longer than you have to be.
    Soon the doctors—hope they are doctors,
    not backwoods undertakers like last time—

will cut letters into your chest.
    They just have to follow the map
    of scars plotted out for them.

But not this time.
    Woke up still in the bag.
    The black plastic cocoon you know

so well. Easy to escape from,
    just push down the zipper
    and out you go.

Don't hear any voices,
    as much a problem as if you did
    hear talking. No voices

might mean you are in the locker,
    flat on your back on a sliding tray,
    heavy door blocking out any voices.

No, it isn't cold enough.
        Not in the locker.
        Still on a gurney,

shrouded in dark,
        waiting for your autopsy.
        Time to get out of here.

The zipper stops,
        you sit up. The room is desolate
        of other living bodies,

population of the dead.
        Some burnt,
        some bludgeoned.

Some you'd rather not think of.
        still have your pants on
        but nothing else.

Have to buy new shoes again.
        Pockets empty, too.
        No shirt, of course.

The paramedics removed it to see
        where you were bleeding.
        Won't be shopping at any convenience

stores for a few hours.
        Shit like this is why you prefer dying alone,
        peacefully.

No one around to steal your stuff
        or carve you open again.

If they only knew you'd been down this road before.
And every time,
  River Styx spits
  you back up on the shore.

You are alive now,
  sure,
  but you'll be

dead
  again
  tomorrow.

Coming Home

"Coming Home" is meant to be read out loud. Watch for the differences in the type and you'll know when to add emphasis. It's fun; give it a try.

This actually happened. My mom and I had taken a road trip and upon arriving home, we found a mouse swimming in the toilet. Little bugger couldn't tread water forever. The moral of the poem is: don't live in a trailer in the middle of the desert.

Mom screams five minutes after we get
        home. *Quick, come see this* she says but she's
        in the bathroom and I don't want to see. She yells
        again so I click off the one channel coming in
        today and walk into the bathroom where

Mom stands, looking at something in the toilet
        now I <u>know</u> I don't want to see whatever it is.
        I almost sat on that she says, pointing at a gray
        mouse paddling its little paws trying not to drown.
        I start laughing and

Mom says *It's not funny. What if I sat down
        and it bit me on the ass?* **What if it did bite**

you I ask **What if it swims there forever?**
It doesn't swim forever—its mousey legs tire,
treading water for another two hours before

Mom flushes the toilet to see what will happen.
The mouse floats awhile before sinking to the
bottom of the bowl. We leave it there, neither
wanting to rescue a rodent corpse out of toilet
water. At midnight I have to shit.

Mom asks the next morning *Did you take it out?*
It isn't there so it must have flushed I say not
thinking about clogged pipes or how a mouse
climbed into the toilet in the first place. Next
time she screams from the bathroom

Mom better not expect me to run.

A Touch of Poe

Imitating Poe is just one of those things most young writers of macabre poetry and stories do early on. It's not as easy as it might sound. Not every poem fits iambic pentameter and can be about dreary midnights and forlorn, grieving lovers.

If you want to, you can rhyme scheme this out. I have some former professors who would have made me do just that during the drafting process of "A Touch of Poe." I, however, wrote this on my own for a Halloween party. It pairs well with Poe's "Ulalume."

The subject matter is, well, its own touch of the legend of Poe.

Was your skin ever so lustrous
Ever so much like the alabaster
Markers leading to this place?

Was your hair ever so perfect
Not a single wayward strand
Breaking the frame around your face?

Were your hands ever clasped
In such silent, pious prayer
Waiting to find Heaven's grace?

133

Were your lips more receptive
More open to mine in the days
Before God took away your taste?

Was your bosom more full
Covered then as now
In your tattered wedding day lace?
Was I ever more ready
To take you in my arms
A cold body in my warm embrace?

Can I still love you
Entombed as you are
In your silken coffin space?

Could you still love me as you are
Shrouded away in this sepulcher
having run your life's race?

Is there still time for us to kiss
Before the sexton comes
And I must not leave a trace?

Pool

I don't write much, directly, about my childhood. "Pool" is a central moment in my early life as far as content goes.

As for structure, the first half is crafted to be like a casting call for a movie. The second half is somewhat of a logline, or the central idea of a movie meant to get producers and directors interested in a project. Successful or not, I am proud of this poem and include it here as one example of how real life can shape creative works.

Casting the movie,
Not of my life but of one event.

Needed:
     woman: 25-30 y/o "Rosalie"
     woman: 23-28 y/o "DeeAnna"
     (should look 3 years younger than first woman)
     Sisters, young mothers

Needed:
     two boys, under eight, should appear six y/o
     Cousins
     "Mikey": blonde/blue

"T.J.": red/blue

Minor character casting to come.
        Let's get these four parts
        first.

Exterior: Southern California
        Every house has a pool.
        Close-up: music swells
        Mikey, tripping,
        can't yet swim and no one there
        to save him

Interior: hospital
        (or home, depending on budget)
        Rosalie calls DeeAnna
        Not what she wants to hear
        No breathing
        No pulse
        Not just sleeping
        Failure to
        resuscitate

Exterior: small white house w/large tree
        DeeAnna can't buy T.J.'s grief
        with Tootsie Rolls
        gooey brown mixing
        with salty tears pooling
        beneath his lip.

The Show Begins at 10:31

After I left the University of Idaho as a student, I answered a bunch of Craigslist ads for writers. I took a few freelance gigs; some paid and some didn't. I found an ad for MatchFlick.com, a North Carolina-based movie website, and pitched them on a recurring horror movie column. The best part about it is that I didn't have to write about new releases. I could riff on whatever I wanted. These columns, written between February and August, 2009, cover a wide variety of topics, including Friday the 13th, malevolent vegetation movies, Rob Zombie, the many incarnations of Dracula, and one on the scariest movie I've ever seen.

It's not about spiders. We talked about that earlier.

During the middle of this run, I had started corresponding with the woman who became my wife. Through her belief in me and a long drive from Las Vegas to Rapid City, South Dakota, I landed better paying freelance work and eventually an honest to goodness job as a journalist. And with that, the column died.

And now, as I find myself in a journalism-related day job again, I have also renewed column writing. The good folks at the Lewiston (Idaho) Tribune spot me a few bucks to write "Unlocking the Vault," a column devoted to sharing the lost pieces of pop culture that have been forgotten. Unlike some pop culture—especially horror— columns, I try to write about things that are still accessible to the average person. I try to write, now, about books, movies, and music that you could pop online or visit a local store and find without too much effort, rather than having to search far and wide for what you want. It's different, but it's fun.

I had fun writing these, too, and they helped keep me sharp between paying gigs.

These columns are dedicated to Joe Bob Briggs.

"Dressing to kill and/or see Friday the 13th"

This column originally appeared on Matchflick.com on February 20, 2009.

Odds are if you are reading this, you've already seen the new *Friday the 13th* remake. You either loved it or hated it. That's how it goes with remakes, especially in horror.

If you haven't seen this, you aren't alone. I'm headed out right now to go stand in line, wearing a T-shirt with the original *Friday the 13th* poster art on it and a hockey mask belt buckle.

I'd be willing to bet that I'm not the only one dressed like this. Someone will have a hockey mask on. Some will have the plain white five-dollar Halloween version, and some will have the "official" mask that is sold by itself or with a plastic machete.

They won't last long. Public places like theaters, malls and, if you are like me and live in Las Vegas, casinos don't take kindly to masked patrons, even for a horror movie.

Look, it isn't our fault that some of us get a bit overzealous. Our heroes just happen to wield dangerous objects and hide their faces. In many ways, it isn't fair. Theater managers don't turn away kids dressed like wizards, do they? You wouldn't refuse to sell a ticket to someone just because they really wanted to be a pirate, would you?

The way it's going, the only acceptable fan costume is to paint your face for the once-a-year showing of *The Crow.*

Any Hot Topic shopper can do that.

I'm a nice guy most of the time, and I wouldn't want to leave you without a solution to this dilemma. Wear the mask. When someone asks you to take it off, do. Trust me on this. Remember the reasons why Jason wears a mask in the first place. Same reason the Phantom of the Opera does.

Do yourself up good. Blood and scars and pus, skin falling off, the whole deal. That person will think twice before asking someone to remove a mask. If that won't work for you or you are going with a group, dress as victims instead. Same concept as the "beneath the mask" gag only without the mask. One thing to remember, however, is to not obscure your vision. You wouldn't want to miss the movie, would you?

If you do dress up (and I do encourage it; if you are going to pay $12 for two hours of entertainment, you should make it an event) you should also consider the concessions. If all you need are a Coke and Milk Duds, you should be fine.

If you are like me, you need popcorn. Preferably popcorn forced to swim in a sea of butter-flavored topping. So much butter that the kernels begin to wilt and your fingers are covered in a greasy residue that is at once irresistible and totally disgusting.

Are you going to wipe that hand on the Jason Voorhees hockey jersey it took you two months to save up for? Are you going to risk having your lard-encased fingers ruining the three-hour makeup job when you have to cover your eyes? Are you going to remember to grab napkins and then not lose them when you set them on the armrest next to you?

Maybe a T-shirt and jeans is the best way to go. Jeans, after all, are nature's napkins. It will be less hassle in the end. You won't lose your place in line; you won't have to worry about someone ruining your makeup if they get scared and choose you to press up against. Popcorn will enter the mouth with no impediments.

Best of all, your secret identity as a masked mass murderer will remain intact. No one ever suspects the person not wearing a mask to be the killer.

"Sean S. Cunningham's best year ever"

This column originally appeared on Matchflick.com on March 6, 2009.

Thirty years ago when the slasher genre crept its way into American theaters, no one thought it would last this long. Even some of its creators assumed it was only of its time and once everyone got over Vietnam it would go away.

They didn't know how right—and how wrong—they were.

Bring us up to 2009. Mired in another unpopular war, oil is out of control, the economy is tanking, and a surprising, young Democratic president is in office. Are you sure it is 2009 and not 1979? Or 1977?

One man was there then and is back again. The reluctant progenitor himself, Sean S. Cunningham. I say reluctant not because he's avoided fan conventions or been out of the movie business but because it seems he's always trying to kill off his hottest property and it never works. Jason Voorhees just keeps coming back.

The last few weeks have been full of news about the *Friday the 13th* remake and its almost $50 million opening weekend. This should be only the beginning of a record year for Cunningham, but it could turn out to be just one good month.

On March 13, which also happens to be a Friday, a remake of Cunningham's first foray into murderous mayhem will be released. Cunningham, along with original writer-director Wes Craven, produced the new *Last House on the Left*.

The biggest difference between 2009's *Last House* and *Friday the 13th* is that I haven't seen any advertising for *Last House*. If I wasn't such a fan of the genre, I might not even know the movie had been made. *Friday the 13th*, however, had massive exposure with prime TV spots and a MySpace push.

So who is at fault for this? Did Cunningham put all of

his energy into *Friday* and let Craven handle *Last House*? If he did, was that really a good idea? Let's look at the records and find out.

Cunningham was a producer of *Freddy vs. Jason*. Whether you liked the movie or not, the box office returns validated its making. Craven was a "based on characters created by" credit. Craven made *Cursed* and has had his name placed on so many bad movies he's getting difficult to take seriously.

"Sean S. Cunningham Presents *Creature From the Black Lagoon*" is not a movie we'll be seeing any time soon, but we have been faced with "Wes Craven Presents *Dracula 2000*." I could gripe about Craven just as long as I could rave about him, but the only bad thing I can think to say about Cunningham is that he made *House II*.

One of the highlights of my DVD collection is the version of *Last House on the Left* with commentary by Cunningham and Craven. They know how to scare people, and they know their history. I'm not surprised that *Last House* is making a comeback now. The original was one of the most brutal films of the 20th century. These two men (along with *Halloween* director John Carpenter) are responsible for the slasher sub-genre. It's a shame that they couldn't get together at the same time their iconic monsters did, but hopefully they were able to shepherd in some of their old magic.

I don't see *Last House* making the same kind of box office bang *Friday* did, and that's just fine. It's a different kind of movie, yet just as right for this time as it was in the 1970s. It is, also, a necessary step in the re-evolution of the horror genre. *Last House* is just as hard to watch as some the current "torture porn" movies like *Hostel* and *Captivity*, but I'm hoping the remake doesn't come off as a sub-par retread.

Like a beautiful woman with ugly kids having cute, but not gorgeous, grandkids.

I also hope that Craven can save the *A Nightmare on*

Elm Street remake from turning out like a burnt turd. I'm starting to wonder if he has any original ideas left.

As for Cunningham, maybe he is outsmarting us all. He's kept his name off projects that would devalue his name (I hate to harp on it, but Craven should have done the same thing), he's kept in touch with the horror genre, and he picked the right time to resurrect Jason and the fiends from *Last House*. Even if Cunningham's March 2009 isn't as good as his February 2009, I'd say it's been a good year for him.

"When plants attack"

This column originally appeared on Matchflick.com on March 20, 2009.

Right now I'm watching *Day of the Triffids*, the 1962 film about alien plant-life bent on devouring all living things on Earth. In many ways, it's a classic low budget flick: better than some, not as good as others. On the other hand, plants aren't scary.

Naturally, I started thinking about other films concerning vegetable vengeance and just what these movies have to say to us in these environmentally-conscious times. Then I started thinking about all the plant movies, like *Triffids*, that are just ridiculous. Ridiculous outweighs poignant by a bushel, with campy classics like *Attack of the Killer Tomatoes* much more revered than *The Ruins*.

Killer Tomatoes and its sequels are prime examples of the chlorophyll carnage cinema. Mutated tomatoes roll through cities, turning people into ketchup. The government intervenes in spectacularly inept fashion, perhaps presaging future federal attempts at defeating entities we do not understand. John Astin and George Clooney appear in sequels. The world is saved, and the argument over tomatoes being fruits or vegetables is laid to rest. Maybe.

The *Killer Tomatoes* movies are not, repeat NOT meant to be taken seriously. If you rent any of them and have friends with significant deficiencies in the humor department, they will ruin the experience for everyone else. Plus, those people shouldn't be your friends anyway.

But when it comes to high camp and pathological plants, the king is still *Little Shop of Horrors*. Whether you choose the original 1961 American International version or the 1986 Rick Moranis musical, you can't lose. The original is much grimmer and lacks a traditional Hollywood happy ending, but it does have a very skinny Jack Nicholson in his first film role. It's brief but is a good indicator of what he would become.

This is the part where I admit that I saw the musical version first. I grew up in the 1980s and was still pretty stoked over Moranis' genius turn in *Ghostbusters*. Every time I am in a dentist's office or someone I know is going to the dentist, I start singing. Just in my head, just in my head.

Oh, no! A triffid attack! Run away from the slow moving Audrey II wannabes. They will eat you alive and not even offer any dinner conversation. Screw the rain forests if this is how they are going to act.

Anyway. *Killer Tomatoes* and *Little Shop* are decidedly on one side of this argument. On the other side are *The Ruins* and *Invasion of the Body Snatchers*.

Hey, pod-people are plants, too. It's either that or the carrot-creature James Arness turns into at the end of Howard Hawks' *The Thing*. That is stretching it too much for me. Ambulatory asparagus and plants that look like people are one thing but shape-changing carrots? I just don't buy it.

At this point in our relationship, do I really need to tell you about *Body Snatchers*? Here's what you do: go over to your grandparents' house and watch it with them. If they start talking about communists and the Red Scare without you saying anything, congratulations. Your grandparents paid attention to the world around them. If, however, they insist that they would have recognized if one of them had turned into a pod-person and the situation never would have gotten out of hand, run. They aren't your grandparents anymore.

Get out while you are still you.

If you survive that, then you can watch *The Ruins*. It's based on a book, which I didn't know until after I saw it. I left thinking two things. First, how could this plot take up an entire novel? Second, how can I use plants that invade bodies to mess with my mom? The first question has yet to be answered because every time I go to a bookstore and remember to look for it, it isn't there, and I don't care enough to look harder and track it down. The second question has been much easier to solve.

All I have to do is get close to my mom and start poking her and saying, "The plants are gonna get inside you, the plants are gonna get inside you," in a very high-pitched voice, not unlike the pseudo-human cries of the vines in the movie.

It's hard for me to say anything bad about *The Ruins*. True, it is a much more serious film than its premise implies. Yes, it is not that far afield from the campy horror of *Triffids*. But I saw it at a second-run theater (yes, with my mom) and only paid $1.25 for the ticket. I got my money's worth. How much did you pay? It has been nine months since I saw *The Ruins*, and I can still scare my mom with that small gesture and stupid voice. I call that a successful film experience.

Day of the Triffids is almost over. The hero just figured out he could stop the rampaging rutabaga with an electrical fence, although he doesn't quite have the power to completely defeat them, just hold them at bay. Then, like early man must have discovered when he became sick of salad, our hero starts a fire. Plants, even those bred on alien Miracle Grow, hate fire. Unfortunately, fire is only a temporary solution. To make a salad really good, you need to add salt.

Much like a side salad, few of these films make for a main course when it comes to horror. *Body Snatchers* aside, plant-attack movies have more in common with junk food. They taste great, but you can't live on them alone. In other words, do not become a movie vegetarian. A horror movie should be a steak dinner or at least a really greasy, undercooked cheeseburger, not a side salad.

"I am Dracula ... and so am I"

This column originally appeared on Matchflick.com on April 3, 2009.

Many men have played the ultimate badass known as Dracula during the course of movie history. Bela Lugosi, Christopher Lee, and Gary Oldman are the three that come to mind first. None of these men were my first Dracula.

When I was five, I watched John Badham's 1979 *Dracula* on a Betamax tape. Frank Langella was my first Dracula. The strange part is that I could only remember one scene, and it gave me nightmares for years.

I remember when Laurence Olivier and Donald Pleasance climb down a wooden ladder into a cavernous dirt crypt and get attacked by a crazy woman all dressed in white with huge fangs and bloodshot eyes.

I didn't know who Olivier or Pleasance were at the time. A few years later, when I saw *Halloween*, I had the strangest sense that I had met Dr. Loomis somewhere. It took me a couple more years to figure out why I thought I knew him.

The thing is, when you are five, you have no way to conceptualize such a scene, let alone an entire film. It is just as difficult to remember a particular actor unless you see them often enough to have his face imprinted on your memory. So the next time I saw Langella, he looked more like that shrieking corpse than the debonair Count. Many would say it's a tragedy that because of these movies, *Dracula* and *Masters of the Universe* are entwined in my memory in ways that I have yet to tear asunder.

On the other hand, how cool is it that Langella has played three of the evilest characters ever created: Dracula, Skeletor, AND Richard Nixon? Somewhere out there, a film student is salivating at the possibilities of a scholarly paper on this.

Eventually, I found the other men who played our Transylvanian friend and discovered that there are better versions of Bram Stoker's classic tale than my first experience. That's how it goes, though. No matter how good it gets later, you always remember your first. Lugosi, Lee, and Oldman are definitely the top of the food chain when it comes to Dracula as a character in our collective memory.

Others like John Carradine, Louis Jordan, and Udo Keir have slipped away from being a part of the mythology. Count Chocula gets more credit for advancing Dracula's persona than any of those three as well as Langella.

When I first read Dracula in my adolescence, it was not Lugosi I saw in my head, even though his is still the iconic image of the vampire. I saw a taller, gaunter gentleman. I didn't hear the Eastern European accent; I heard a light British accent, almost indiscernible from the voice of my own thoughts. I was convinced there were fangs when there were none.

And I expected a giant hook on a ship to hoist Dracula to the sun and away from his prey. It isn't bad to have one's expectations unmet.

Badham and Langella's *Dracula* is not the best film version of the story ever made. As an adult, I know this. I know that the best Dracula movies are Francis Ford Coppola's *Bram Stoker's Dracula* from 1992 (Oldman and Sir Anthony Hopkins more than make up for Keanu Reeves and Winona Ryder) and Werner Herzog's *Nosferatu* (yes, I think it is better than F.W. Murnau's silent film) also from 1979.

Klaus Kinski had that same bug-eyed insanity that Kier had in *Andy Warhol's Dracula* and combined it with a suffering that would not be seen in the character until Oldman took on the role.

There is not enough room here to go over the entire list of actors who have played Dracula. I could try to rank them, but what would be the criteria? Would it be a ranking of "who did it best" or "these are my favorites," two lists that could start a fight, if I wanted to do so? Would I throw in good performances from bad movies, like Richard Roxburgh in *Van Helsing* or Gerard Butler in *Dracula 2000*? What about actors in movies for younger audiences, like Duncan Regehr in *Monster Squad* or, hell, Count von Count from *Sesame Street*?

They all bring something different to the role, from the absurd to the transcendent. Langella, however, will always be my Dracula. Like I said, you never forget your first.

"Christine overdrive"

This column originally appeared on Matchflick.com on April 17, 2009.

I'm getting a new car this week. It's a scary thing. I've always driven other people's cars or been a passenger. If I told you how old I was when I finally got my driver's license, you'd probably laugh and wonder how I ever survived in the world. The car, of course, isn't new, really, but it is twenty years newer than what I have been driving for the last three years.

What does this have to do with movies, you ask? In many ways, nothing. In others, a lot. My movie choices are influenced by what is going on in my life, sometimes in disjointed ways, sure, but I always make it work. So right now, I am watching *Christine*, and later I'm going to watch *Maximum Overdrive*.

I will attempt to set my undying (though not unwavering) love of Stephen King aside, but I make no promises.

There is little doubt that *Christine* is the better of these two films. Directed by John Carpenter and starring no one who became famous, it is a classic high school horror movie. If you were the nerd who restored a hot rod just to get laid, this is your movie. If you were one of the bullies who trashed the nerd's car, feel lucky that cars don't actually come back to life on their own.

Wouldn't that be great, though? Never have to pay a mechanic or get an oil change. Break downs on the side of the road wouldn't happen. You'd just get to cruise, and all it takes is premium gasoline and a human sacrifice every once in a while.

The iconic image from *Christine* is of the 1958 Plymouth Fury running down a mook while engulfed in flames. Headlights beaming vengeance, windows tinted so dark the stunt driver doesn't exist, and all that fire: from the hood, from behind the wheels, from the back. If ever there was a hell-car, Christine is it.

The movie isn't perfect, but if we are judging on the standards of Stephen King adaptations (*The Shawshank Redemption* and *The Green Mile* being at the top and *Children of the Corn* sequels being at the bottom), then *Christine* is definitely in the top ten percent of the galaxy of King films.

Not so much for *Maximum Overdrive*, King's first and only directorial effort. It is universally panned as a bad movie and even more so for King's attempt to direct it. And yet, I love it. I know it is a bad movie; I know Emilio Estevez is not an action star; I know someone ripped off a giant Green Goblin head for the "leader truck"; I know all of that and more.

I also know that King himself has said it was a bad idea and that he was drunk and coked out the whole time. So, really, is it his fault that *Maximum Overdrive* sucks harder than a brand new Hoover?

Undying love, here we go.

I say, no. He was making millions of dollars at the time and someone (Dino De Laurentiis, to be precise) decided to spend the dough to let him have a go at directing. It didn't work out, and everybody knows it. So leave the guy alone. If *Maximum Overdrive* shows up on your late night cable, you don't have to watch it if you don't want to.

But why not give it a chance, huh? Do it for me. If nothing else, just watch the first twenty minutes or so, just to see soda machines pop out cans like missiles, lawn mowers cut more than grass, and electric knives get skittish. Do it for the AC/DC soundtrack.

Do it just to watch one of cinema's best lines ever.

Our humble director appears early in the film, wearing a stupid hat and his very own Coke-bottle glasses. He walks up to an ATM during the initial bout of machines going crazy. The screen reads, "You are an asshole," then repeats the epithet. Without missing a beat, King turns to his movie wife sitting in their station wagon and says, "Honey, come on over here, Sugarbuns. This machine called me an asshole."

I love it. No lies. I'm laughing right now because it is so damn funny. Yeah, OK, the rest of the movie blows massive chunks, but it is far from the bottom of the barrel when it comes to King movies or movies about possessed motor vehicles.

Just for fun, go ahead and watch *Christine* and *Maximum Overdrive* back-to-back. I promise it will be great. If you do, I want you to do me a favor. While watching *Maximum Overdrive*, I want you to pay close attention to the prologue statement about the meteor. If you notice what I notice, try telling me there isn't a little of Stephen King that's psychic.

Just try to hold onto your lunch when you see those 1986 gas prices.

As for me, by next week's column, I'll be cruising in my new car. Maybe I will name her Christine, just for fun.

"All epidemics start somewhere"

This column originally appeared on Matchflick.com on May 1, 2009.

A potential global epidemic of swine flu is breaking out all over the news. OK, I know, it's serious. People have died, lots more are sick. So what better way to escape the horrors of real life than by watching a scary movie? And why not watch one that relates to the current world conditions?

There are many options. You could watch *28 Days Later* or its adequate sequel *28 Weeks Later*. You could rent the recently released *Quarantine* or search around for its superior Spanish version *[Rec]*.

The ultimate globe-spanning flu movie is the miniseries of Stephen King's *The Stand*. I think you know about me and Steve, so I will spare you (for now) from more of my idol worship. Instead, I want to tell you about a little movie you've probably never seen.

In 1985, a film crew set up shop in the small town of Payson, Utah. Actually, it was the second time in two years that Hollywood came to visit. Remember *Footloose*? This time around, however, Hollywood wasn't interested in teen rebellion, dancing, or a kick-ass soundtrack. This time, they came to ask what would happen if an accident happened at a biological weapons laboratory.

What's that? You've heard that plot before? Of course you have. Films like *Outbreak*, *28 Days Later*, and *Resident Evil* have all explored what happens to the world in these situations. In *Warning Sign*, the difference is that the plot is contained (pun intended) within the building itself, and the small town sheriff tries to save the people he knows who are trapped inside.

Much like in *28 Days Later*, the virus in *Warning Sign* makes people crazy and violent. Most of the deaths in this mostly goreless film are due to an infected person killing someone else. In one memorable shot, a guy in a hazard suit swings an axe at Kathleen Quinlan. I remember how his eyes looked like they were about to burst.

I was five. These are the things you remember.

I also remember one shot of a mob outside the building (a building very, very close to my grandparents' house, by the way). The camera pans the building, sort of a mob's-eye view. As more of the crowd is taken in, a head of curly red hair appears, nearly filling the screen.

That head, folks, is my mom. That's right; my mom was in a horror movie. Sure, it's a subpar film, but go back and look at that list of movies that, in one way or another, ripped off its plot. Serious actors came out to be in the movie, too. Besides Quinlan, Yaphet Kotto had a major role, and Sam Waterston played the sheriff, looking for a way in, when everyone else wanted out.

Tragically, I haven't seen *Warning Sign* in many, many years. We'd rent it if we saw it at a video store, but never looked hard enough for a copy to buy. I think it is on DVD now. I should poke around for a copy, for two reasons. First, it captures Payson at a time in my childhood that reflects my memory of it. So does *Footloose*, but in a totally different way. If you visited Payson now, the recognizable landmarks from both movies are almost all gone. The ones that remain are surrounded by new houses, new businesses, and new people.

Do you think other people get as nostalgic as this? Maybe all the people who go to Astoria, Oregon, for the *Goonies* conventions understand.

The second reason I need to get a DVD copy of *Warning Sign* is that last week was my mom's birthday. That would have made a pretty good present, I think, especially since I can't give her back the town of her youth, let alone the town of mine.

Now that I think about, *Warning Sign* isn't even that scary. I do believe it has a place in the pantheon of outbreak films. Sure, its premise was already trite in 1985 when it was released, but at the time, AIDS was just being recognized as a deadly disease, and *Resident Evil* wasn't even a dream. People were still playing "Pac-Man" and "Asteroids."

I loved "Asteroids." I wasn't very good, but that didn't matter because it was fun and provided a good memory. Just like *Warning Sign*.

When all is said and done, more people will probably get swine flu than have seen *Warning Sign*. That should be a good excuse to go out and watch it. You know, before you get sick and can't do anything. Let me tell you, if you do get sick, watching *Warning Sign* is the last thing you will want to do.

"Drag me to lunch with Sam Raimi"

This column originally appeared on Matchflick.com on May 15, 2009.

I saw *Army of Darkness* before I saw the other two *Evil Dead* movies. Does that make me a bad person? Do I lose any street cred just because *AoD* had a major theatrical release, and I was able to catch it when it came out and then went back to see all that came before? Do I lose even more points because I saw *Darkman* before any of the *Evil Dead* movies?

Could be worse. I could be one of those people who didn't know who Sam Raimi was until *Spider-Man* came out. Or, gods forbid, *For the Love of the Game*.

Lucky for you, I'm not one of those people. As you can imagine, I am disgustingly excited for Raimi's return to horror, *Drag Me to Hell*.

I have a stack of preview articles about the film, and I haven't read any of them. I want to be surprised. I want to be caught off guard, like I was when I finally saw *Evil Dead*. I miss that feeling. It's something Raimi is good at, like when *For Love of the Game* turned out to be a decent film. And how *Spider-Man 2* felt more like an *Evil Dead* movie than a comic book sequel, sans gallons of fake blood.

Some of the hype I haven't been able to avoid tells me that *Drag Me to Hell* will satisfy my fake bloodlust. The hype also informs me that I should be pleased with the film, if for no other reason than that I am a Raimi fan. This bothers me. It could mean two things. It could mean that I will be surprised and engrossed (and grossed out) by what the movie has to offer. It could also mean that whatever level of auteur filmmaking Raimi has reached could have degraded into self-parody.

Raimi, as you may know, forged his career on a sort of self-parody. After all, *Evil Dead* was just a remake and feature-length version of *Within the Woods*, the profits from which financed *Evil Dead*. And (stretching into obvious territory here for anyone who has seen these movies) *Evil Dead 2*, for all intents and purposes, is a remake and lengthening (and extended mythologizing) of *Evil Dead*.

In other words, if anyone can successfully repeat himself, it's Raimi. Only now, he doesn't have to beg for money or cast only his friends.

I'm sorry. I don't think there will be a Bruce Campbell cameo in *Drag Me to Hell*. If there is, sweet. Bruce is the man. If The Chin or Raimi's brother Ted (you know, the nerdy guy who always has at least one line in every Raimi picture and spent a lot of time with Hercules) doesn't show up, I will get over it if the movie fulfills the rest of its potential.

There's no reason it shouldn't. Raimi hasn't exactly shied away from the horror genre. He and producing partner Rob Tapert did put up the dough for the American version of *The Grudge*. Their Ghost House Pictures has managed to bring many independent horror films to U.S. audiences, both in theaters and direct-to-DVD. Raimi knows what he is doing; he knows where the horror genre has been and is, and has only become a better filmmaker in the years since he had to run his own camera and drive that yellow Oldsmobile.

Hey, wouldn't that be great? How about a shot of the Olds, just to really bring things full circle? C'mon, Sam, we're your friends. Give us what we want.

Oh, wait. Maybe that's why *Drag Me to Hell* even exists. Raimi really does love us and has not forsaken us for the glamorous world of record-breaking box office receipts. That's a nice thought. On the other hand, maybe Raimi is a selfish bastard and made the movie for himself, just to prove that he hasn't become a tool to the will of the major studios. Sounds like a damn good reason to me. I have a feeling that if Raimi is happy, we will be, too.

Or maybe he just wants to swallow my soul. Maybe he told someone else why he made the movie, and I just haven't read it yet because I don't want to read anything about *Drag Me to Hell* until after I see it.

Sam, call me. Let's do lunch. I know some good places in Las Vegas.

"Home is where the horror is"

This column originally appeared on Matchflick.com on May 29, 2009.

I want you to tell me a haunted house story. Don't start with "there was this family" or "this group of people got together" or anything like that. Don't take too long.

You can't do it, can you? I couldn't either. I could not think of one haunted house story, novel, or film that didn't involve a family or group of some kind. There is a simple explanation for this: it would be boring.

Imagine it, if you will. One person, alone in a house, all manner of supernatural activity occurring, ghosts aplenty, and . . . what? Where's the drama? The house drives the one person bonkers, and he or she is just another ghost. Boring.

When you get more than one person, say, a struggling family with a diverse range of weaknesses to exploit, and throw them in with poltergeists, well, now you are cooking. That is where the magic happens.

So a film like *The Haunting in Connecticut* relies on the unity and hardships of the family to succeed. If we believe in the family, we can believe in the ghosts. The other class of haunted house movies, the "random group brought together for various reasons" kind, lacks that immediate bond and is rarely as satisfying. There are superior examples, though. Robert Wise's *The Haunting* stands as the epitome of the subgenre. Too bad its modern remake with an all-star cast can't be locked away like a dirty secret, never to be seen again.

The random group movies spend too much time with quirky connections to be truly satisfying. The groups are never completely random. The participants are brought together because some psychic researcher wishes to exploit their gifts (*The Haunting, Rose Red*) or because they all have secret needs from one person (*The House on Haunted Hill*). These films attempt to offer a broad range of characters so that audiences can choose with whom to identify. The filmmakers seem to miss the key point of the family-oriented haunted house. Everyone has a family, or at least knows one.

This is why movies like *The Others* and *The Haunting in Connecticut* can succeed with little to none of the tricks other horror movies use. At the very center of these films is the ideal of the family unit and how outside forces break apart families. This is also why the best of the group-oriented haunted house movies were made in the 1950s and '60s. Hollywood had not yet approached the taboos of divorce, abuse, and alcoholism in its horror films. The monsters were still out there, ready to be met by explorers into the unknown. Once Hollywood broke through and realized all the worst of the monsters were inside the home, they didn't need to throw together groups of strangers who just needed to survive one night. They had everything they needed in the modern American family who had to stay because they couldn't afford to move.

Of course, Hollywood is nothing if not original. This is why screenwriters and producers scoured newspapers and books for "true stories" to turn into movies. In the process they created a stew of conventions no haunted house story would be complete without.

Was your house built over a cemetery, preferably a Native American burial ground? Congratulations, your house is probably haunted.

Did the previous inhabitants of your house die in a gruesome manner, perhaps at the hands of another family member? Better move, your house is haunted, too.

Were any sort of strange rituals performed in the home, including, but not limited to, séances, exorcisms, torturing of witches/pagans, sacrifices to the devil, or voodoo? Yeah, you should have U-Haul on speed dial because you may need to leave your house in a hurry. Before it collapses into the tainted ground it stands on.

Then again, none of that matters until just the right family moves in and is ready to confront the ghosts. If we learn nothing else from movies like *The Amityville Horror* and *Poltergeist*, we should at least know that blended families with alcoholic dads will always be driven apart (usually with sharp objects) and that young families with cute little blonde girls tend to attract the wrong crowd.

Speaking of *Poltergeist*, is anyone else as surprised as I am that the preacher-ghost wanted poor little Carol Anne and not her brother? Must not have been Catholic.

That's the other thing: you rarely see a truly weak family at the center of one of these movies. They always pull together at the end and somehow make it through. Especially if there's going to be a sequel. Also just as rare is the family that stays in the house after everything happens, even if they "win." Who'd want to stay in a place where chairs stack themselves and the trees are alive? In the case of *The Haunting in Connecticut*, the house gets burned down, so the family couldn't stay if they wanted to.

Besides, the main kid's cancer gets cured anyway, so there's no reason for them to stay in Connecticut.

Did I ruin the ending for you? Worry not, you can catch it all again on the Discovery Channel or on DVD soon. After all, it is a true story. They have the whole family ready to back it up. Because that is what families do, and it takes a lot of ghosts to break that apart.

"Universal's forgotten fiend"

This column originally appeared on Matchflick.com on June 12, 2009.

I was in a second-run theater not long ago and had some time to kill. I strolled into the arcade and had to decide between the only two games I am any good at: a first-person shooter or pinball. The pinball machine available was *Universal's Monster Bash*, so naturally I drifted that way. I played, did OK, and then saw the movie I was there for. It wasn't until a few days later that I noticed something odd.

Not long after exhibiting my limited pinball wizardry, I found a copy of *The Invisible Man: Complete Legacy Collection* DVD for a very reasonable price. That's when it hit me. One hardly ever sees the Invisible Man with the other monsters. And not just because he's invisible, either. It's almost like he's been forgotten. If you asked me if the Invisible Man is on the Universal Monsters logo, I'd have to say no. He should be, but in my memory, he's just not there.

This could easily become the most stupid pun-filled column I have ever written, as you may have noticed. I'm going to try to avoid that. All the puns I could come up with are glaringly obvious.

In the matter of *The Invisible Man*, James Whale's 1933 film, calling it a classic would be an understatement of the highest order. Deciding what else to say, though, gets more difficult, so I will stick to just a few key elements.

Claude Rains. That's right. It's all about the voice when it comes to playing the Invisible Man. The legend goes that Whale agreed that Rains' lone screen test up to that time was awful when it came to acting, but his voice was perfect. Rains was a nobody with no Hollywood experience, and if it wasn't for *The Invisible Man*, audiences quite possibly could have been deprived of his talent forever and been none the wiser.

Just for a second, imagine *Casablanca* without Claude

Rains. Sure, they would have found someone else for his role, but with Rains in the film it becomes complete. Once again, Hollywood has horror to thank for getting one of its best actors his first starring role.

Now for a word on the groundbreaking special effects: awesome.

What? You need further explanation? You want to know how, in 1933, they turned a man invisible on the screen and made it look reasonably realistic? Sorry. I'm not telling. Not my job to reveal the secrets of moviemaking. I prefer to maintain as much of the magic as I can. Just watch the movie and figure it out for yourself. Or get the same DVD collection I bought and watch the bonus documentary. Like most of the *Legacy Collection* sets, the much too short documentary on this one was written and produced by David J. Skal. When it comes to the history and analysis of horror history, Skal is the man. I bow to his superior knowledge. I also quote his work whenever it seems appropriate.

We've talked about Rains and the special effects, but what else makes the Invisible Man a classic able to hang out with Dracula, the Frankenstein Monster, the Wolf-Man, and the rest of the gang? He's been mentioned before.

If you haven't seen *Gods and Monsters*, get off your butt and go get it right now. I will wait.

Oh, good. You're back. So now that you've seen *Gods and Monsters* (which mostly focuses on the making of *Bride of Frankenstein* and rightly so), you have seen that Whale was a freaking genius. You might also start to wonder why his name never comes up when it comes to lists of horror directors, especially who is and is not a "master of horror."

Tod Browning comes up all the time, and many critics (those contemporary to him and those of today) consider him a hack. Hell, how many people think of Edward D. Wood, Jr., before James Whale when asked to name a horror director from the days of black and white?

Too many, that's how many.

Whale was too good for his own good and managed to avoid being tagged as simply a horror director. Yes, his career eventually stalled and he committed suicide, but you already knew that because you just watched *Gods and Monsters* like the good little ghouls and boos I know you are. If you haven't yet, just go along for now and correct your egregious error as soon as you can.

So, three things, that's all you need to know about *The Invisible Man* and why you should watch it: Claude Rains, excellent special effects, and James Whale. One would think that would be enough to get higher billing than the Creature from the Black Lagoon, but no. It even got to be in *Monster Squad*. Where was the Invisible Man?

He was probably right there, going unnoticed, just waiting for the right time to say hello. Either that or he was still in seclusion after having seen Chevy Chase in *Memoirs of an Invisible Man*.

"The scariest movie of all time"

This column originally appeared on Matchflick.com on June 26, 2009.

People often ask me what the scariest movie I have ever seen is. They say, "Hey, T.J., what scares you? Please tell us."

For a long time, I had to stop and think about it. I hadn't been legitimately scared by a movie since I was a kid. What scared me then is not necessarily what scares me now, although I know for some people it is. When I was five, what scared me the most was the library ghost in the opening of *Ghostbusters*. I screamed; I ran; I hid behind a curtain, barely peeking through the opening. Eventually, I knew what was going to happen and made it through the rest of the movie. Nothing is as bad as that for me, when it comes to a pure jump-scare moment.

Then I got old (as opposed to growing up). I've seen a lot of horror movies, and I can honestly say most of them don't scare me. I watch other people get scared, and I laugh. When the monsters come out, I laugh. That is my response. It is a pleasurable feeling. I laugh like a maniac on roller coasters, too, and have occasionally found myself standing near the coasters in Las Vegas, grinning at the sounds of people screaming in fear and joy.

But I'm not scared. I'm not afraid of spiders or snakes or chupacabra. I'm not afraid of werewolves or vampires or mummies. The truth is, only one thing really scares me: women. And the scariest of them all, all-time for me, isn't Glenn Close in *Fatal Attraction*, Sharon Stone in *Basic Instinct*, or the Angelina Jolie computer animated version of Grendel's Mother in *Beowulf*. It's cute, little, innocent Ellen Page in *Hard Candy*. Sure, she's an indie darling now, and everyone loves her. She still scares the crap out of me.

When people ask me that question, the one about what

scares me, that's not really what they are asking. They are looking for a recommendation. They want me to tell them what I think will scare them. So I say *The Exorcist* or *Dawn of the Dead*. They don't want to know that I am afraid of a teenage girl. I have to really know a person to recommend *Hard Candy*, which is sad because it's an amazing film. It is tense and suspenseful. The direction by David Slade is superior to his efforts in his follow-up *30 Days of Night*. *Hard Candy* is also an editing gem, with 99 percent of the violence and anything truly disturbing (or illegal) happening off-screen. Hitchcock would be proud.

The script and the performances bred from it are also far better than much that comes out of the horror genre. Properly, *Hard Candy* isn't even really a horror movie, but it is scary enough to be one.

In terms of plot summary, Page plays Hayley who meets Jeff, played by Patrick Wilson (you know, Nite Owl from *Watchmen*). He's a late 20s fashion photographer, and she is a teenager. They meet up and go to his house. At first, it looks like poor Hayley is about to be the victim of a pedophile, but the tables are soon turned and turned again. Much mayhem and some surgery ensue until both are pushed over the edge.

Deciding who is predator and who is prey is part of the genius of the film. Jeff may or may not be innocent of the previous violations against a girl Hayley knew. If he is innocent, then we should be on his side, hoping Hayley stops herself before she goes too far. If he is guilty, he deserves everything that Hayley can dish out. As for her, either way she won't be able to go back to being an innocent little girl. She may avoid becoming a sexual victim, but the mental and emotional turmoil she endures (much of it of her own making) will scar her for life.

And that is what scares me. Not only am I afraid for this girl and what could happen to her physically, I am also afraid she will become a worse monster than she thinks Jeff is. I am on her side, but it is different than cheering for a slasher like Jason Voorhees. For most of the film, Hayley feels the remorse that a creature like Jason does not. Yet she proceeds to carry out her plan. It is also difficult to be on her side because, well, I'm a guy. No man wants to imagine the girl behind the counter at Burger King coming for his balls just because he was maybe a little too flirty.

As such, it is easier to stay opposed to Jeff. Innocent or not, he brought an unaccompanied minor he'd never met before into his home. It is difficult to believe he had only the noblest of intentions. He is a monster of his own sort, perhaps not fully formed yet but on his way. In serial killer parlance, Jeff has killed a few stray cats and been in a fight or two but hasn't killed a person yet. At least, that is what he tries to convince Hayley of. As far as she is concerned, he's diddled her entire high school home economics class and is going to pay. In the end, no one wins.

What makes *Hard Candy* the movie that scares me the most is that it is 100 percent plausible. There are super intelligent girls like Hayley out there, and it will only take one pervert for them to focus that intelligence and turn it into something cruel and remorseless. When I first saw the movie, I avoided eye contact with any woman who looked under 20, which was hard because I worked at a community college bookstore that was also next to a high school.

You never know which girl is going to go berserk because you looked at her wrong, so it was just best not to look anywhere. I memorized a book's worth of cloud shapes in two weeks.

So next time you ask me what movie scares me the most, make sure that is what you want to know. Much like *Hard Candy*, the answers can be difficult to swallow.

"Camcorder carnage"

This column originally appeared on Matchflick.com on July 10, 2009.

If you've ever watch your home movies from the pre-digital 1990s, you know how scary they can be. Hours of relatives making stupid faces, telling bad jokes, and pretending to be camera shy. All you wanted was for someone to get hit in the crotch so you could win $10,000 from Bob Saget. Maybe you got lucky and captured a lightning strike or a dog chasing its own tail.

We won't talk about your attempts at amateur pornography.

It's amazing to think that someone actually made any money with a camera they bought with daddy's credit card, but it has happened. Forget the short films you made in high school. Yes, those were a necessary step in your filmmaking evolution, but they weren't "the show." Now remember how pissed off you were ten years ago when you saw *The Blair Witch Project* and said to yourself, "I could have made that."

You didn't. I didn't, either. I used my Panasonic VHS camcorder to tape weddings and goof off. We all need to get over it.

I won't lie to you. I bought the hoax. The first bits of footage I saw were too real not to be trusted. It wasn't so much naïveté as it was my desire to believe. I was not alone.

By the time I saw the film in the theater, I knew it wasn't real, but I didn't care. I loved it, and I was angry when some of my fellow movie-goers stood and yelled at the screen.

"That was the stupidest thing I've ever seen," I remember hearing. There weren't as many swear words as one might think. I did see it in Utah. The disappointment of half the crowd threatened to surpass the quiet excitement felt by the rest of the crowd. I couldn't breathe after the final frame.

I sat, listening to the slurs directed at the film and trying to hear if my heart was still beating.

I went again a week later. I would have called it déjà vu, but I wasn't surprised by the outcome.

Another admission: I went to *Blair Witch 2: Book of Shadows* on its opening night. Please, don't think less of me for it. It wasn't a waste of time, but I should have gone to a matinee. I've only watched it once since then, and I still like it. I'm not rushing out to see it again.

Since *The Blair Witch Project* became the ultimate indie success story, I've been waiting for a film to capture that same magic. Something in the herky-jerky handheld images appeals to me. Combine that with the best excuse to keep action off screen (always remember, what you don't see is worse than what they can show you) and it's a winning formula for me. No one had been able to do it, much to my dismay.

One last guilty plea. I didn't see *Cloverfield* when it was released. I was in the middle of a self-induced protest against PG-13 horror movies, and I was practically broke. I had to choose what movies I saw with more discretion than I would have liked. It was not until Tuesday night that I finally saw *Cloverfield*.

Cloverfield = off screen action + handheld images + one camera = winning formula.

Notice something in that equation? Unlike *The Blair Witch Project*, which combined film and video, *Cloverfield* is shot from a single camera. It builds on the POV shots of films like *Peeping Tom* and *Halloween* and runs wild with it. If our humble cameraman Hud doesn't see it, neither do we. In fact, we only see Hud's face three times in the whole movie.

One of those times is when he dies. The rest of the time we only get his voice, which sounds to me a lot like Jason Lee. I half-expected him to show up in some two-minute cameo, Kevin Smith-style.

I also kept waiting for the tape to run out or the battery

to die. Apparently, camera batteries last longer than cell phone batteries. I'd like to know what kind of camera they used. It can support ELP tapes (hence the implied seven hours from start to finish), has a decent light on it, and has night vision.

Night vision? If my camcorder had night vision capabilities, I'd have a lot more footage of things that go bump in the night.

Not that kind of bumping, you sicko.

Now I'll just have to wait for the first successful movie shot entirely with an iPhone. It could happen. Perhaps one of you has already started it.

"Hit the road, Jack"

This column originally appeared on Matchflick.com on July 24, 2009.

The lure of the open road calls to the summertime American like few things in our culture. Strange roadside attractions, cheap greasy food, and radio stations that lose their signals during your favorite song are all part of the mystique.

So, too, is the dark side of road trips.

There is always the possibility that a deranged, faceless trucker will stalk you for 500 miles like in *Duel*, the 1971 debut of Steven Spielberg. Grand Master of horror Richard Matheson wrote the screenplay based on his own story. Right from the beginning of his career, Spielberg knew suspense and tension. He holds out on us the entire length of the movie, never revealing the face of the truck driver. This turns a dilapidated Peterbilt into one of the scariest villains ever. If you've ever had a large truck behind you on a two-lane highway, you know how Dennis Weaver felt in *Duel*: scared out of your mind.

I might be courting danger, but I have the recently released audio version of *Duel* ready to go on my iPod. Tragically, half of my trip will be on blank, mindless interstate. Any semis on the road will be able to pass me without a problem.

Apparently, J.J. Abrams thinks truckers are scary, too. One of his early writing credits is the 2001 Paul Walker film *Joy Ride* (also known as *Roadkill*). I saw this when it was released. Walker was hot after *The Fast and the Furious*, and Steve Zahn stars as his quirky brother. I like Zahn. He makes me laugh. Walker, on the other hand, is a stone. I cheered for him to get caught by the mad trucker they pissed off by fooling around on a CB radio.

I might have to watch *Joy Ride* again. I just looked at a

plot synopsis that states the two brothers are driving from Colorado to New Jersey. Below that, two actors are listed as playing characters from the Salt Lake City Police Department. Last time I checked, Utah was not on the way to Newark from Colorado.

Proving that Abrams is not the only Hollywood success story to start with a really crappy road movie, the 1991 cable staple *Highway to Hell* was written by Oscar-winner Brian Helgeland. Gives a guy hope.

You've probably seen *Highway to Hell* and didn't know it. I didn't the first time I saw it. For years I thought it was called *Hell Cop* or *Piece of Crap with a Certain Charm*. The original vampire-slaying Buffy, Kristy Swanson, is in it. She plays a girl who is kidnapped by the Hell Cop to be the next bride of Satan (or Beezle, in the film), played by Patrick Bergin.

It gets better. Richard Farnsworth, Lita Ford, Gilbert Gottfried, and the Stiller clan (Amy, Jerry, and Ben) all make cameos. Ben Stiller appears as Attila the Hun, and Gottfried plays Hitler.

Highway to Hell isn't a road movie in the same sense as *Duel* or *Joy Ride*, but there is a journey with a purpose, and I think that's all that counts. It does incorporate the single basic premise of a road horror movie: interruption of the trip. My favorite interruption is The Creeper from *Jeepers Creepers*.

Admit it, you try to figure out the vanity plates you see. Some of them are crazy, some are lame. BEATNGU is a classic. I've always wondered, though, how did The Creeper get a vanity plate? Did he apply for it himself, or did he steal it from another car? Creeeeeeeeeppppyyyy.

In addition to some great effects, a badass creature, and the introduction of Justin Long, *Jeepers Creepers* also sports one of the all-time great final frames. The Creeper is sewing, there's some screaming, and, of course, "Jeepers Creepers," that old standard from the 1930s. The camera pulls back and we see Long's skin, minus the eyes. Roll credits.

Brilliant.

With that in mind, I'm hitting the road. I have my *Duel* reading, plenty of road music, and maybe even a CB. I know some people who would not like it if I had my own road horrors, but I am hoping for some adventure.

If you never see this column again, you'll know something happened. Just kidding. I'll be fine.

"Feeling (Rob) Zombiefied"

This column originally appeared on Matchflick.com on August 7, 2009.

Halloween will come early again this year, thanks to rocker/director Rob Zombie. His sequel to his 2007 remake of *Halloween* comes out later this month. Instead of getting into the pros and cons of remakes (again), I'm just going to talk about Zombie.

One could spend a lot of time discussing the imperfections of Zombie's work as a director. One could say he spent too much time explaining Michael Myers, that he ruined the notion of evil without cause or justification. OK, I can buy that. The difference is that Zombie chose to make his own movie. He did his job, as opposed to just recasting and reshooting the film, like Gus Van Sant did with *Psycho*.

Getting into childhood trauma may not have been the boldest move Zombie made, but it works for me for a couple reasons, and both are performance-related.

As the ten-year-old Michael, Daeg Faerch is complex and frightening. He hates everyone except his mom and his little sister. He isn't the totally silent, heartless killer that the adult Myers is. He is still a sad and confused boy, and it's easy to see how the isolation of institutionalization contributes to his further receding from the rest of the world.

Sheri Moon-Zombie gives the other performance that makes the first half of the film worth watching. She plays the role of conflicted mother to perfection. She's angry at Michael for killing the rest of the family (sans little sister), but is still mommy, wanting to comfort and support her troubled child. She should be playing more serious roles in serious films, but will probably never get the chance to prove it in more serious roles.

The rest of the movie plays out more like John

Carpenter's original. Tyler Mane is a big, scary dude, and the teen scream princesses are adequate in their roles. Some of them even get to return for the sequel, which Zombie said he wouldn't be making upon the first film's release.

This isn't Zombie's first sequel, of course. His first two films, *House of 1000 Corpses* and *The Devil's Rejects*, make an interesting pair. I've said it a million times, but it bears repeating: *House* is a nightmare fantasy, and *Rejects* is what happens when those people wake up. *House* even has the look of a dream compared to the gritty reality of *Rejects*. This theory also makes it easier to reconcile the inconsistencies, such as recasting and relocating, from one film to the next.

Zombie's growth as a screenwriter and director is easy to see. When watching *House*, you can see how new he was at the process, yet comfortable with the ideas. He knew what he had and thought he knew what he wanted to do but didn't have the muscle to fight a Hollywood studio like Universal. When it came time to make *Rejects* with Lionsgate, Zombie got to make the film how he wanted to and had learned from his experience making *House*.

Zombie has an advantage over many other modern horror film directors in that he has surrounded himself with good influences. He made one of the fake trailers in *Grindhouse* for Quentin Tarantino and Robert Rodriguez. Like Tarantino, Zombie has an extensive knowledge of genre film history and is almost as good at finding the right music for the right moment. If one didn't know better, *The Devil's Rejects* could have been a Tarantino film. Zombie also has a flair for resuscitating stalled careers by casting icons like Bill Moseley, Sid Haig, Ken Foree, and Tom Towles.

Between sequels and remakes, it might start to seem like Zombie doesn't have an original idea to his name. Thankfully, that's not true. The animated film *The Haunted World of El SuperBeasto* will finally be released in late September, and *Tyrannosaurus Rex* is in pre-production.

Zombie has always had a flair for the theatrical, having been influenced by Alice Cooper and Kiss. His visual style has transferred well to the screen, and it will be exciting to see what else he can do. I think some time off just to write will be good for him and for horror fans.

Like Something Out of Stephen King

I started reading Stephen King when I was eleven years old.
Misery *was my first, and somehow I still wanted to be a writer. I didn't understand everything or every word in the book, but I knew I liked it. I knew that somehow I would find a way to make other people feel like King made me feel: scared, excited, anxious, and filled with limitless possibilities.*

As I went through higher education, I tried to finds way to discuss King on the same level that my colleagues were discussing Herman Melville, Philip Roth, Walt Whitman, and a slew of other canonical literary figures. It wasn't easy. The following paper was written for the Advanced Literary Theory and Criticism course during my first year of grad school. Later, I was able to present it at the Popular Culture Association's national conference. That trip took me to New Orleans, a city I had wanted to visit since picking up Anne Rice and Poppy Z. Brite in the years following my discovery of King. The highlight of the presentation was meeting one of the eminent King scholars, Tony Magistrale, and hearing him say only good things about what I had written.

I know that for many writers, and especially those working in the horror genre, high-end literary criticism and theory are neither interesting nor relevant to their work. I can respect that. For most literary scholars,

*the horror genre is junk. I have a harder time respecting that opinion
and am doing what I can to change it.*

In the world of popular American literature, there is
arguably no name bigger than Stephen King. Since the release
of his first novel *Carrie* in 1974, there has rarely been a year
without a new King book, and, invariably, these books reach
the bestseller lists. But Stephen King has not always been a
household name. He has not always been America's
boogeyman. His rise to fame in the world of American
letters, however, is not the journey I will be tracking here.
Rather, I will seek to discover how Stephen King became
Stephen King. More than just an author, King has become a
brand, a subgenre unto himself. King can also be read as text.

Like the work he has produced, King is wrought with
connections: from text-to-text and author-to-text. King is not
only self-referential within works bearing his name, but has
referenced himself in books published under a pseudonym,
and has even become a character. Like Michel Foucault, I will
not be "examining how the author became individualized in a
culture like ours…" (904), but rather exploring "the
relationship between text and author and with the manner in
which the text points to this 'figure' that, at least in
appearance, is outside it and antecedes it" (904).

Yes, there was a Stephen King before there was *Stephen
King*, but by delving into a sampling of the overall text under
that name, we will see not only how an author can transcend
his own work, but also how the work, the text, can transcend
the author.

In 1983, not yet a full decade into King's career as a
published author, he was invited to speak at the Billerica,
Massachusetts, Public Library. As would become common of
his public speaking engagements, King anticipated one of the

questions. "Of all the questions I'm asked, the most difficult is, 'How does it feel to be famous?' Since I'm not, that question always catches me with a feeling of surrealism," King said early in his talk (Underwood and Miller 1).

At this point in his career, King was still making the attempt to be just a regular person. Yes, he had become rich in the preceding years, but he did not consider himself "famous." King still had a modicum of the Foucauldian ideal of an author's role. "[T]he mark of the writer is reduced to nothing more than the singularity of his absence; he must assume the role of the dead man in the game of writing," Foucault wrote in "What Is an Author?" (905).

There is difficulty in seeing King in *Carrie*, a short novel about high school girls which includes many instances of epistolary storytelling. There is no burgeoning alcoholic father of two (eventually three), struggling to pay the bills by teaching high school English and publishing short stories in men's magazines. There is no son yearning for a father figure. There is, in fact, very little in *Carrie* of what would soon become recognizable as being written by King. The novel does take place in King's native state of Maine, and the book is the story of a misunderstood outsider and the horrible things that can happen when one person is treated poorly by so many.

King, in his memoir *On Writing*, recognizes this absence: "For me writing has always been best when it's intimate, as sexy as skin on skin. With *Carrie* I felt as if I were wearing a rubber wet-suit I couldn't pull off" (76). King pushed through his struggles, completed the book, and was on his way to becoming *Stephen King*. Yet this requires us to look back to Foucault and ask another one of his questions. "Even when an individual has been accepted as an author," Foucault said, "we must still ask whether everything that he wrote, said, or left behind is part of his work" (905).

The same year as his speech at the Billerica Public

Library, King was the subject of a *Playboy* interview in which he says *Carrie* was "often clumsy and artless" but that the book allowed him escape "into a totally different existence" (Underwood and Miller 33). That new existence would be King writing horror novels about writers.

King, for all intents and purposes, created the sub-subgenre of horror novels featuring a writer as the central character. Often, when we think of Stephen King, it is such a novel that we picture. But this can be misleading. Of fifty-four novels published between 1974 and 2013, only twelve feature either a writer or some other type of creative artist as the central character or a major secondary character. Granted, a few of King's novellas and a fair number of his published short stories feature such a character, but to make the assumption that this is the only type of lead character he has produced is a mathematical falsehood. Yet, when we think back to Foucault's question and our popular conception of King as an author, should we be only considering those texts which seem to fit together as the text of Stephen King?

The problem with doing this is that those novels (and for this paper, let us focus solely on the novels) in which a writer is the central character are perhaps King's most disconnected works. Yes, there are thematic connections: issues regarding the creative process, obsession, family, the intrusion of the past into the present, and, of course, death can all be found in this quarter of King's work. One could argue that it is in these individual works that the overall text of Stephen King was created. We must, as Foucault demands, determine what constitutes a work and therefore the complete text of Stephen King.

We could easily leave *Carrie* out of the discussion if we were to solely look at those works containing a male writer as the protagonist. But by doing so, we would be forced to ignore *The Stand*, *The Dead Zone*, *Pet Sematary*, and *The Green Mile*, all of which have at different moments been called

King's best work. We could, if we wanted to be so simplistic, equate characters with their creator, and even King himself has offered such a chance.

In his memoir, he speaks about his own battle with alcoholism and how his family had a habit of keeping themselves to themselves: "Yet the part of me that writes the stories, the deep part that knew I was an alcoholic as early as 1975, when I wrote *The Shining*, wouldn't accept that. Silence isn't what that part is about. It began to scream for help in the only way it knew how, through my fiction and through my monsters. In late 1985 and early 1986 I wrote *Misery* (the title quite aptly described my state of mind), in which a writer is held prisoner and tortured by a psychotic nurse. In the spring and summer of 1986 I wrote *The Tommyknockers*... (96)

The Tommyknockers is about a writer (in a rare move for King, a female writer), who discovers an alien craft and is granted strange powers from the craft. "What you gave up in exchange was your soul," King writes. "It was the best metaphor for drugs and alcohol my tired, overstressed mind could come up with" (97).

As appealing as this invitation to correlate the "real life" of the author with the fictional lives of his creations is, it can be just as misleading as assuming King only writes about writers. David H. Richter, in his introduction to the work of Kenneth Burke, provides Samuel Taylor Coleridge as an example. Burke, according to Richter, equates Coleridge's albatross to Sarah Coleridge and refers to "The Rime of the Ancient Mariner" as "Coleridge's symbolic way of purging the guilt arising out of his failed marriage and his drug addiction, and of achieving an equally symbolic redemption" (634).

As King points out for himself, the alcoholic, failed writer Jack Torrance in *The Shining* is King working out his fears of becoming a monster to his children (Torrance dies). *Misery*'s Annie Wilkes, the nurse who imprisons Paul Sheldon, her favorite writer, is the drugs and alcohol shackling King and forcing him to produce work he may not want to be producing (Wilkes dies and the book Sheldon writes for her is destroyed). And Bobbi Anderson, the heroine of *The Tommyknockers*, after experiencing the most prolific period of writing in her career, is killed by her lover Gard because she is out of control and assisting in the alien takeover.

Addictions, in these novels, do not necessarily lead to the death of the addicted, and King himself has survived his own addictions to drugs and alcohol. But, as previously stated, making these types of biographical connections is not always the best means of examining a text's relationship to the author, even if said author has laid bare those connections himself. Not every writer in King's work has such an addiction. Bill Denbrough, for example, grows up to be a horror writer in the novel *It* but doesn't suffer from any chemical dependencies. Mike Noonan, the hero of *Bag of Bones*, similarly does not have a chemical dependence. Scott Landon in *Lisey's Story* does exhibit many symptoms similar to King's dependence, but, like Denbrough, Landon's issues have more to do with childhood trauma. And so we see that, perhaps, there are other ways to group King's novels together: some thematic or by character-types, and sometimes just from the classifications provided by the author himself. It is in this last area, a classification provided by the author both explicitly and implicitly, that truly pushes King out of the realm of author and into the realm of text.

We can easily group a section of any author's works together if we are explicitly told each work is part of a series. We know that *The Hobbit* and *The Silmarillion* are related to the three books of *The Lord of the Rings* without much effort. We know that King's *Dark Tower* series consists of eight novels and one novella. A common core of characters and a series-spanning narrative (*The Wind Through the Keyhole* and *The Little Sisters of Eluria* are out of the timeline, but still part of the canonical series) immediately show readers that these books belong together. But it is not the enclosed nature of a long series with a beginning, a middle, and an end (which readers of the series will know is not so simple) that makes *The Dark Tower* the preeminent text of Stephen King the author and Stephen King the idea, but rather its connections to other individual works in the oeuvre of King and King's inclusion of himself as a character.

Before the publication of *The Dark Tower VI: Song of Susannah* in 2004, in which King first appears as a character, he had made references to himself and his other works a handful of times. Some of the references made sense. Early novels set in the fictional towns of Castle Rock and Derry, Maine, often refer to events and characters from previous books, but this is basic world-building. The stories rarely impact one another.

In the novel *Thinner*, published under King's pseudonym Richard Bachman, King places his work as part of the fictional world of the book. At one point, the main character Billy Halleck refers to his supernatural situation as being like something from one of King's novels. It is a subtle moment, but one in which we can see King's awareness of himself as an idea to be referenced and used in a fictional manner. References to other novels are peppered throughout *The Dark Tower* series but become particularly noticeable in the fourth book, *Wizard and Glass* (1997), when the main characters walk into a scene from *The Stand* (1978). In 1994, Roland, the last Gunslinger, would make a brief appearance in *Insomnia* (the protagonist of which later meets Mike Noonan at a café in Derry). But it would not be until the publication of *The Dark Tower V: Wolves of the Calla* in 2003 that these seemingly random connections would begin to be more than just happenstance.

In King's second published novel, *'Salem's Lot*, one character disappears after confronting the vampires of the novel. Father Callahan, deeming himself to be unclean after being forced to taste the blood of the vampire Barlow, leaves town and is never heard from again. Fans questioned this for years, wondering about the fate of the brave but weak clergyman. More than twenty years later, Father Callahan would resurface as a character sucked into the world of Roland and his friends. This was a welcome return and filled in the years since Callahan last appeared on the page. But there was more to it. Late in the novel, Callahan and the group discover a copy of *'Salem's Lot* which includes Callahan as a character. After being read portions of his own life, Callahan reacts accordingly, exclaiming, "But this is a novel! A novel is fiction! … Damn it, I'm a REAL PERSON!" (708 original emphasis). King is mentioned as the author of the novel, and the seeds are planted for his appearance as a character.

The character "Stephen King" appears at various moments in *Song of Susannah* and *The Dark Tower VII: The Dark Tower*, coinciding with the author's actual life. Roland and Eddie Dean first find the fictional King in 1977, before the serial publication of *The Dark Tower: The Gunslinger*. King, the character, is shocked to see his creations before him, but not entirely. During this meeting, Roland determines that King is not a god and had abandoned the story of the gunslinger. The possibility of the story remaining unfinished would become a key theme not only in the life of the author but in the arc of the King character as well.

This story, the moment when King becomes more than just an author, begins on June 19, 1999. King is walking on the rural highway near his home in Maine when he is struck by a van. "There is a break in my memory here," King claims in his memoir. "On the other side of it I'm on the ground, looking at the back of the van, which is now pulled off the road and tilted to one side" (254).

King elaborates, weeks into his recovery, telling us what

we have already assumed: "[I]t occurs to me that I have nearly been killed by a character right out of one of my own novels" (256).

Before moving into a comparison of this scene from King's memoir to the fictionalized version he would give readers in *The Dark Tower*, it is worth noting the frequency of similar car accidents in other King texts. If we ignore the more traditional vehicle-on-vehicle accidents such as in *The Dead Zone* and focus instead on vehicle-pedestrian or single-car accidents, we see a startling pattern. We must, also, look solely at works written before the summer of 1999. The most obvious novel to consider in this regard is *Christine* (1983), as its title character is a malevolent Plymouth that runs down numerous characters. Paul Sheldon, the writer in *Misery* (1987), wrecks his car in a snowstorm and suffers broken legs not unlike those suffered by King during his accident. In *Thinner*, Billy Halleck unintentionally kills a gypsy woman who was crossing a street. Bill Denbrough's stutter in *It* (1986) supposedly began as the result of a car accident that occurred before the events of the novel. And perhaps most horribly, young Gage Creed is killed by a semi-truck barreling down a rural Maine highway in *Pet Sematary* (1983).

There are more car accidents—and vehicular homicide is the topic of King's most recently published novel *Mr. Mercedes*—but the pattern is there if we choose to look for it. Does it mean that King predicted his own accident? Certainly, it does not. But these instances do reinforce the idea of King as a text to be taken as a whole and not just as an author entirely absent from his work as Foucault would have us do. What King has done is build the mythology of himself into his works and made King the man and King the idea inseparable.

King's writing process is part of the scene in *The Dark Tower* just prior to the accident. King, the character, is thinking instead of a walk, he should be home, maybe working on the next installment of the series in which this scene takes place. He's reminding himself not to make up too many words for his fantasy world. Roland and Jake, the young boy who has been part of this story since the first volume, are trying to track down King in order to save him from the accident. They, and the readers of *Song of Susannah*, have been told that King dies on the nineteenth day of June, 1999, before he can finish Roland's story.

They save him, but not without sacrifice. Jake takes the full brunt of the impact, pushing King out of death's grip by only inches. Jake, whom Roland let perish in book one, dies again. King, in writing himself as a character, filled in the gaps of his memory with perhaps his greatest character, Roland. In the blackness, King speaks with Roland and is urged to finish the tale to see the wheel of Ka make its full turn. King would take another five years to finish the three books (*Wolves of the Calla*, *Song of Susannah*, and *The Dark Tower*) that would, quite literally, bring the story full circle. And in that time, the text that is Stephen King would only grow.

King began to give the number 19 significance in the final books of *The Dark Tower* and this, to him and his publishers, warranted a revision of the first book of the series (books two, three, and four were left untouched). In the text of King, this was not unusual. He had replaced a large portion of text, revised, and republished *The Stand* in the late 1980s. An illustrated version of *'Salem's Lot*, which including "deleted scenes," was released in 2005 (after Father Callahan's story was completed).

But how are we to read these texts? Are they to be considered the canonical versions? Should we, remembering Foucault, consider everything ever written by an author to be a "work" and included in the text of an author? In the cases of *The Stand* and *The Gunslinger*, many readers do not have a choice but to accept these revised editions. Original versions of these two texts are out of print. Yes, one can still find copies of the originals (this author owns a paperback of the original version of *The Stand*, purchased at a yard sale for fifty cents; hardcover copies of the original version can sell upwards of $1500 if in good condition), but any reader new to King's work would be required to put some effort into finding an unrevised text. One could argue that this is solely influenced by the market, that King has, in fact, become something more than just an author. King was aware of this quite early in his career.

A 1980 essay titled "On Becoming a Brand Name" deals with this very topic: "Being a brand name is all right. Trying to be a writer, trying to fill the blank sheet in an honorable and truthful way, is better. And if those two things ever change places on me (and it can happen with a creepy, unobtrusive ease), I'm in a lot of trouble" (qtd. in Spignesi 111).

King's switch from mere popular author to greater idea was permutated by the marketplace. Even today, new horror authors are invariably compared to King. King himself writes blurbs for authors who have been called "the next Stephen King." Whether any of these authors transcend the notion of being just an author, as King has, remains to be seen.

Stephen King, more than just an author, has become fixated in American literature as an idea. While he has yet to reach the adjectival status of H.P. Lovecraft (although some of his own works have been called "Lovecraftian"), King represents a known commodity, even when the works themselves defy expectations through plot and characters. We can open a Stephen King novel and know that there is a decent—but not overwhelming—chance that the main character will be a writer; we can take comfort in waiting for someone to be hit by a car; and we can read carefully, watching for those moments when one book connects to another which connected to yet another work in the vast library that is the text of Stephen King. Whether we consider his works as a whole or choose to disregard some individual texts (as far too many readers have done with *The Dark Tower* series), we must recognize that King represents more than just the actual physical being writing in Maine (or Florida, as has been the case in recent winters).

This idea was not formed solely by the popular consciousness, but by the author himself from the first time he mentioned one of his books in another right through the fictional recounting of his own near-death experience. As King continues to add to the vast work he has produced (King has released five books since this paper was first written: The Bill Hodges trilogy featuring *Mr. Mercedes*, *Finders Keepers*, and *End of Watch*, the novel *Revival*, and the short story collection *Bazaar of Bad Dreams* with two collaborative novels due in 2017), readers will be looking for connections to the greater text at hand, no matter how minute those connections are.

Works Cited

Bachman, Richard. *Thinner.* New York: NAL Books. 1984. Print.

Foucault, Michel. "What Is an Author?" David H. Richter, ed. *The Critical Tradition.* White Plains, NY: Bedford/St. Martin's. 2007. Print. 904-14.

King, Stephen. *The Dark Tower V: Wolves of the Calla.* Hampton Falls, N.H.: Donald M. Grant. 2003. Print.

_____. *The Dark Tower VI: Song of Susannah.* Hampton Falls, N.H.: Donald M. Grant. 2004. Print.

_____. *The Dark Tower VII: The Dark Tower.* Hampton Falls, N.H.: Donald M. Grant. 2004. Print.

_____. *On Writing: A Memoir of the Craft.* New York: Scribner. 2000. Print.

Richter, David H. *The Critical Tradition.* White Plains, NY: Bedford/St. Martin's. 2007. Print.

Spignesi, Stephen J. *The Lost Work of Stephen King.* New York: Citadel Press. 1998. Print.

Underwood, Tim and Chuck Miller, ed. *Bare Bones: Conversations on Terror with Stephen King.* New York: McGraw-Hill Book Company. 1988. Print.

Her Name was Maybe Amber

Las Vegas, here we come! I met my friend William, whom you will read about in "Her Name was Maybe Amber," in Anthropology 101 at the Community College of Southern Nevada. I don't have to tell you much about him because you'll get enough when reading this piece. It is enough for me to say that he was one of those people who strayed into and out of my life that I will never forget.

"Her Name was Maybe Amber" is a hybrid work. For many people, that can mean a mix of fiction and creative nonfiction, or a prose-poem. I tried something different. My hybrid mixes creative nonfiction and screenplay styles. Like most hybrids, it is experimental. The challenge was knowing when to move from short screenplay descriptions and into longer prose sections. The natural fit for the style I attempted here is dialogue. If nothing else works in this, the dialogue, in form and content, is spot on.

You should read this and listen to the music of Richard Cheese and Lounge Against the Machine. It is quintessential Vegas music with a delightful twist.

EXT. – Spearmint Rhino—Las Vegas—Dawn

William, 30, long brown hair, clean-shaven, high-priced shirt and jeans, exits the Spearmint Rhino Gentlemen's Club with T.J., 25, red hair, glasses, scruffy beard, and rumpled clothes. The sun has just topped the Vegas strip high rises.

WILLIAM
Do you have the keys?

T.J.
Why would I have your keys?

INT.—William's silver Dodge Stealth

Close up on William's keys, lodged between the driver's seat and the center console.

PAN TO: William, hands cupped around his face, pressed against the driver's side window.

WILLIAM
I see them.
(He stumbles away from the car)
I can't believe I left my goddamn keys in the car.

T.J.
(Too tired to laugh)
I can.

WIPE CUT (like a Kurosawa movie):

Let me bounce this off you. That was William's phrase for every idea he had. As in, "Let me bounce this off you. How about we come back to the lot tonight and I let you practice driving my car?" Or, "Let me bounce this off you.

How about after class we go down to the Centerfold and see what happens?" The problem was that I didn't have a driver's license and was not going to joyride in William's sleek sports car. The other problem was that I never had any money and the Centerfold Lounge had a two-drink minimum.

The Centerfold also had Las Vegas's worst strippers, which is why it was in Henderson and why it was torn down shortly after I left Vegas. So when William bounced the idea of one long night of clichéd Las Vegas debauchery, I had a hard time saying yes. I had a harder time saying no.

William had a coupon for a new club. No cover charge and one free drink. The catch was that you had to arrive in your own car. We had parked back at the Rhino (hours before discovering the keys were still inside), had a few drinks at a nearby bar, and decided to walk over to the new place. For some reason, walking didn't count and so our coupon was not honored. Not surprisingly, the club was dead. Midnight on a Thursday is not a happening time, even in Las Vegas. But the party never ended for William, which meant we were both too drunk to walk back to the Rhino.

EXT.—strip club whose name I can't remember—midnight

T.J.
We should get a cab. Do you see any?

WILLIAM
No, but I can go use the phone inside.
(William takes out his wallet, stuffed
with cash and business cards.)

A VOICE
Hey, you need a ride?

PAN TO:

A white, two-door Chevy Cavalier pulls up next to us. A stout man with a blonde crew cut and an implacable accent asks if we need a ride. He's a cab driver, just off shift and headed home. If it's close by, he'll give us a lift. William, knowing no strangers, puts his wallet away and opens the passenger door. He climbs into the back seat.

"We're trying to get back to the Spearmint Rhino," William says and introduces himself. The driver, Peter, shakes hands and peels away from the curb just as I am shutting the door. My knees are pressed against the dashboard. William and Peter are talking about the various clubs and which one has the best titties. Peter, we learn, is a Russian from Cuba. He moved to the island from Leningrad with his parents when he was ten. And now he drives a cab in Las Vegas.

In just a few minutes, Peter will almost get us killed.

CUT TO:
INT.—T.J.'s memory—early morning

Once, just once, I went to the Centerfold Lounge by myself. I was depressed because it was my birthday. Or maybe it was my birthday and I just happened to be depressed. I could easily get to the Centerfold from my house, and I had some birthday cash. I sat at the rail, in the same seat I always sat in. I ordered my two Smirnoff Ices and prepared to get boobs rubbed in my face.

The first dancer out was a familiar one. Ann or Amber or whatever she'd chosen for her stage name. She was one of the better-looking dancers at the club: average height, cropped brunette hair, almond eyes, and an oddly alluring shark's smile. She grinned and waved at me, then shimmied her way to my seat and bent over, ass in the air for the patrons on the other side of the catwalk.

INT.—Centerfold Lounge—Henderson, Nevada—9 p.m., Halloween 2005

AMBER (or maybe ANN)
Where's your asshole friend?

T.J.
I don't know.

AMBER
You're better off without him.
(Amber finishes her set. Two more dancers come and
go as T.J. sinks into thought…)

She was right and wrong. William was bad for me. I drank more and went to strip clubs with him. By myself, I didn't drink much or go to strip clubs—except this once, give me a break, it was my birthday. What she didn't know was that every time I tipped her a Lincoln, it came from William. We were good cop, bad cop. He'd tease dollar bills at the girls and I would throw down fives on the second song. I rarely spent any of my own money.

The scary part is that I still don't know what William did for a job or where all that money came from. It wasn't my business to know how he could blow $300 in ninety minutes playing blackjack. I know that he had once been a massage therapist, had dropped of the University of Miami, was from New York, and almost got a Mötley Crüe tattoo for his eighteenth birthday. I also knew that he had a good heart.

CUT TO:
EXT.—SUNSET STATION—Henderson—Oct. 23, 2004

WILLIAM

We need to save a spot for Karen.

                          T.J.
                Who? She your girlfriend?

                       WILLIAM
                She's a bigger Alice Cooper fan
                 than you are, that's who she is.
              She's easy to spot. She's in a wheelchair.
                       Just look for her.

PAN TO:

     KAREN, mid-30's, wheelchair-bound due to multiple
sclerosis. KAREN is not WILLIAM's girlfriend; she is his
patient. He drives her around when she needs to get places
and is her massage therapist. KAREN wears a billowy black
lace top, a black leather skirt, dominatrix boots, and a slash of
crimson lipstick. As she propels her wheelchair toward
WILLIAM and T.J., WILLIAM elbows T.J. in the ribs.

                       WILLIAM
                  Don't stare. It looks like
                 You're staring at her chair.

                        KAREN
         (One hand steering her chair, the other raised, with
                  index and pinky pointing.)
                    School's out, boys.
                      Let's party.

CUT TO:
EXT.—Bus stop across the street from the Centerfold
Lounge, Halloween 2004.

     I didn't stay long that night. I drank my drinks and left,

more depressed than before. Not six months later, I was in a stranger's car with WILLIAM, hurtling toward certain doom and the Spearmint Rhino.

CUT TO:
EXT.—Las Vegas—late night

White Chevy is stuck behind a line of cars, waiting for a train. PETER, the driver, is visibly upset, shaking his fists, pounding them on the steering wheel. He rolls down his window.

INT.—White Chevy—late night

PETER
(shouting out his window)
Move your fucking ass, asshole!
(to WILLIAM in the backseat)
You see how these people drive? Always
in the way. No courtesy for anyone.
(Out the window, again)
You fuck, fuck you!

CUT TO:

I blame the train. If we hadn't been stuck in the middle of a pack of cars while a freight train rumbled through the city, we might have entirely avoided death instead of brushing by it. Peter, who had proven to be a frightening driver, had no patience. He had to get us where we were going now. Being a cabbie, he knew a short cut.

Honks from the cars behind us as Peter worked his way into a zig-zagging U-Turn didn't stop him. Neither did the median island. Or the oncoming traffic he turned into without stopping. It could have been worse. The train blocked off more cars from careening into us. Peter's reflexes kept his car from scraping the retaining wall on the passenger side and the other cars on the driver's side.

I managed not to scream, but I had sobered up, fast. After driving about seven blocks out of the way, we were on the other side of the train and soon at the Spearmint Rhino.

CUT TO:
EXT.—Spearmint Rhino—Las Vegas—even later at night

A small crowd of men hover near the doors. A bouncer in a white shirt and black suit watches everyone. A red carpet leads to the door, making everyone who enters feel important. It doesn't help ease the cost of drinks at the establishment. Like every Gentleman's Club, there are rules:

Check your ID at the door.
Accept a pat down from the bouncer.
Do not touch the girls.
Two drink minimum.
Water is not free. (They don't tell you this one until you try to cup a handful of water from the men's room sink.)

I don't remember much from the next five hours. I might be the only man in the history of men to have fallen asleep inside one of the most famous strip clubs in the world. Gene Simmons, I'm sorry. Turns out I can't rock and roll all night and party every day. When William tapped me on shoulder, I thought I had only dozed off for a few minutes. Miraculously, he had decided it was time to go. He said something about breakfast. But it was too early for breakfast, I thought.

EXT.—Spearmint Rhino—Las Vegas—Dawn

T.J.

(voiceover)

The sun hits me hard, like the traffic we narrowly
avoided the night before. The parking lot is empty,
except for William's Stealth. He reaches into his pocket
and…

WILLIAM

Do you have the keys?

DISSOLVE TO:

EXT.—near the Las Vegas Strip—early morning

WILLIAM and T.J. walking to a 24-hour adult
bookstore to get a phonebook and look up a locksmith.

T.J.

Dude, I can catch a bus here and head home.

WILLIAM scowls. They enter the bookstore.

CUT TO:

INT. – Dodge Stealth—early morning

WILLIAM

(driving)

Let me bounce this off you.
Let's go back to my place
and crash for a while.
We'll get some breakfast and
go see *Sideways* at the Orleans.

T.J.

I thought you'd seen that?

<u>WILLIAM</u>
Yeah, but it's great.

CUT TO:
INT—theater at the Orleans Casino—late morning

The theater is empty except for WILLIAM and T.J. Neither looks like he's been home since the day before. They both smell like makeup foundation, alcohol, cheap perfume, and sweat.

<u>T.J.</u>
You know that one dancer at the Centerfold?
Ann or Amber or whatever her name is?
She thinks you're an asshole.

<u>WILLIAM</u>
Good. I prefer it that way.

CUT TO:
INT—T.J.'s memory, present day
<u>T.J.</u>
(Voiceover)
Let me bounce this off you.
If you ever see William, and you'll
know if you do, remind him not to
lock his keys in his car.

FADE OUT TO:

THE END

About the Author

T.J. Tranchell was raised in Utah and lives in Moscow, Idaho, with his wife, Savannah, and their son, Clark. He holds a Master's degree in literature from Central Washington University and is the author of *Cry Down Dark*, a novella. In 2017, he attended the Borderlands Press Writers Boot Camp lead by Tom Monteleone.

Tranchell has been a journalist, a grocery store janitor, a customer service clerk, and occasional fast food employee. He has found his place in writing fiction and teaching English and journalism.

Asleep in the Nightmare Room is his second book.

Author photo by Melissa Hartley